THE VAMPIRE MOVES IN

Angela Sommer-Bodenburg
pictures by Amelie Glienke

Dial Books for Young Readers
E. P. Dutton, Inc. / New York

First published in the United States 1985 by
Dial Books for Young Readers
A Division of E. P. Dutton, Inc.
2 Park Avenue
New York, New York 10016

Published simultaneously in Canada
by Fitzhenry & Whiteside Limited, Toronto
First published in English in 1982.
This translation © 1982 by Andersen Press Ltd.
First published in German in 1980
as *Der kleine Vampir zieht um*
by Rowohlt Taschenbuch Verlag,
Reinbek bei Hamburg, West Germany
Translated by Sarah Gibson
Design by Nancy R. Leo
Printed in U.S.A.
First Edition
COBE
10 9 8 7 6 5 4 3 2 1

Library of Congress Cataloging in Publication Data
Sommer-Bodenburg, Angela. The vampire moves in.
Summary: Banished by his family for making friends with a human,
a little vampire turns to Tony, his only friend, takes up residence
in the basement of his apartment building,
and makes chaos of Tony's life.
[1. Vampires—Fiction.]
I. Glienke, Amelie, ill. II. Title.
PZ7.S6966Vam 1984 [Fic] 84-7062
ISBN 0-8037-0077-6
ISBN 0-8037-0078-4 (lib. bdg.)

Excerpt from "On Top of Spaghetti," song by Tom Glazer,
© Songs Music, Inc., Scarborough, N.Y. 10510. By permission.

This book is especially for Katja, who played with her cuddly
animals all the time I sat at my desk—and for everybody whose
vampire fangs have already grown, and for those, like Burghardt
Bodenburg, who are still waiting for them.

Angela Sommer-Bodenburg

Contents

1 / Terror in the Tub

Tony Noodleman was lying in the tub, reading *In the House of Count Dracula,* when the front doorbell rang.

Hope it's not for me, he thought, looking up from his book. He heard his mother open the door and then come back across the hall to the bathroom, where she knocked.

"Someone to see you."

"Oh, Mom, I'm reading," grumbled Tony. "Who is it?"

"A vampire."

"A vampire?" He was so startled he nearly dropped his book in the water. But on second thought, his mother must have been joking, because *she* didn't believe in vampires, even though she had recently met two of them. Both she and Tony's father believed that Tony's two new friends, Rudolph and Anna, with their moldy, smelly vampire capes, were simply a couple of children who had spent a little too much time dressing up in their grandmother's clothes. And Tony figured it was better to keep the truth—that he had started hanging out with two real live vampires—to himself. So he merely asked cautiously, "Which vampire is it?"

"Rudolph," came the answer.

That gave Tony another scare. Something terrible must have happened to knock all the energy out of Rudolph. Otherwise, why would he have just come over the way most friends did, appearing at the apartment's front door, instead of making his usual dramatic entry through Tony's bedroom window?

"Just a minute, I'm coming," he called, clambering out of the tub.

In the hallway stood the little vampire. He looked gray and hollow cheeked, and his little red eyes flickered feverishly.

"I have to talk to you," he whispered.

Tony gulped. "Here?" he asked incredulously, turning his head toward the living room, where his parents were sitting.

The little vampire looked at him with soulful eyes. "You *must* help me," he whispered. "You're my only friend."

"I am? Oh. Well, um, how—?" stuttered Tony.

2

"Come down to the basement as soon as you can."
With these words, the little vampire turned around
and disappeared.

"Has he gone already?" called Tony's mother. "I
was just getting some juice for you."

"He doesn't like it," said Tony, who was preoc-
cupied with other thoughts. How in the world was he
going to get away with going down to the basement
at this time of the evening?

While he was getting dressed, he announced casu-
ally, "I'm going downstairs for a minute."

3

"What? Now?" exclaimed his mother. "Your hair's all wet. Has this got anything to do with your funny friend?" she asked suspiciously.

"No," fibbed Tony.

"Why do you need to go out, then?"

"To bring in my bike."

"Your new bike?" Dad's voice joined in now. "Do you mean you left it outside, and all this time you've been relaxing in the tub?"

"Sorry." Tony hid a smile, knowing very well that his bicycle had been safely locked indoors for the past two hours. "I'll be right back."

Grinning, he shut the front door behind him and pushed the elevator button. What a big deal about a lousy bike. All he needed now was for Dad to call after him, "Don't forget to lock up!" The elevator arrived and Tony got in. On the way down, he remembered how exhausted and depressed the little vampire had seemed. His high spirits dwindled. What could have happened to make Rudolph come to the apartment like that for help? What if the nightwatchman had discovered his family's vault, and Rudolph was the only survivor? Tony's heart began to beat more quickly. That would mean that Anna, Rudolph's little sister . . . No! Vampires were not beaten that easily, and especially not by old Mc-Rookery. Tony had to admit, however, that he was by no means harmless—Rudolph had already told him of McRookery's ambition to have the first vampire-free cemetery in America. By this time, Tony had reached the basement. He opened the door of the elevator and listened—not a sound. Cautiously, he took a couple of steps, then turned on the light. The basement hallway was empty, the door to the bicycle rack shut.

Slowly he moved forward till he came to the door. He stopped and listened again. Nothing to be heard. He took a deep breath and turned the handle. At once, he was met by a familiar smell: a dank odor of coffins and decay.

"Rudolph?" he called hesitantly.

"Psst!" It came from the darkness. "Come in and shut the door."

2 / Banishment

Just before Tony closed the door behind him, the light from the basement hallway revealed bicycles leaning against one wall and a large box—on which were sitting two shadowy figures. Then everything got dark, and it took a couple of minutes before Tony's eyes adjusted themselves to the pale light that filtered through the two tiny windows. Now he could see that the two figures were wearing capes. Their faces were pale and ghostly. Both were vampires. The smaller, slighter one could only be Rudolph—but who could the second, stronger and bigger one be?

"Rudolph?" said Tony uncertainly.

"Yes," came the reply. "Why don't you come and sit down?"

"Where?"

"Here, on the coffin with us."

"Coffin?" So the large box was a coffin. A terrible thought occurred to Tony. Supposing the coffin were for him? He'd read lots of books about how ordinary people were turned into vampires....

"Come on!" called Rudolph impatiently.

Knees knocking, Tony groped his way over to the coffin and sat down on the very edge.

"Is something bothering you?" asked Rudolph, laughing.

"I—er . . ."

"He's scared." The second figure spoke, and the grating voice sounded sort of familiar. "He doesn't know what to expect."

"I have to be getting back," said Tony.

"Did you tell them where you were going?" asked Rudolph sharply.

"N-no," stammered Tony.

"Good." Rudolph sounded relaxed once more. "I'll tell you what this is all about." He paused. Tony tried to get a look at the second vampire, but couldn't be sure who it was.

"Listen." Although everything was quiet, Rudolph's voice sank to a whisper. "I left home. I've been banished from the vault."

"Banished?" Tony didn't understand.

"Yes. I'm not allowed to go back there anymore."

"Why?"

"Because I've made friends with humans. That's strictly forbidden for vampires."

"How did they find out?"

"From Aunt Dorothy. She's been sniffing around on my trail for weeks. She put the whole thing before the family council and they forbade me to go back to the vault."

"That's not fair," said Tony angrily. "Where are you going to live?"

Rudolph gave a little cough. "Well, here, with you, I hope."

"With *me*?" Tony was horrified. "How in the world do you think you can do that? First of all, my parents—"

"Oh, I don't mean in the apartment," interrupted Rudolph. "I mean down here, in the basement."

"But anyone can come in here!" Tony threw a despairing look at all the bicycles propped against the wall. "People need to get stuff, like their bikes."

Rudolph gestured impatiently. "Not *right* here. I mean in the locked-up storeroom that belongs to your apartment."

"You can't!" Tony was beside himself. "My mom and dad would find out right away."

"No, they wouldn't. Not if you were smart," said the second vampire.

"What if my mother needs something from down here, like wine?"

"You'll have to get it for her," came the croaking reply.

"And if my father wants to do some carpentry?"

"Distract him. Turn the T.V. on, or buy him a sports magazine."

"My father doesn't like sports magazines," said Tony.

"He wouldn't. Well, you'll just have to think of something else. You're not that stupid."

"Okay, okay," said Tony quickly, to avoid rubbing him the wrong way any further. Maybe he was Gruesome Gregory, Rudolph's elder brother? He was just as bad tempered as this, and Tony got the creeps whenever he thought of him.

"What about the coffin? You're not thinking of keeping that here too?" he asked Rudolph.

"That's the most important thing. Where else would I sleep? Or did you think we'd dragged it all the way over here just for fun?"

"Oh, um, no, of course not—it's just that the storeroom's kind of full and . . ."

"We'll just have to make room for it, then," declared Rudolph, and stood up. The second vampire slid off the coffin too.

"What are we waiting for?" he growled.

"I—I don't have the key," said Tony. "It's upstairs. I didn't realize . . ."

"Well, go and get it," ordered the larger vampire. "And hurry up."

"Okay," said Tony, stumbling to the door.

Tony ran through the basement to the elevator. What reason could he give his parents for having to go back down to the basement again? Maybe he could just try to sneak in and out of the apartment unnoticed? But he'd already been out for way too long, and if he didn't show up soon, they were sure to come downstairs looking for him. He'd better start thinking up some story. He felt relieved once this was decided, and took the elevator up to his floor.

"Tony?" called his mother as soon as he had unlocked the door.

"Yes?" he answered in his most cheerful voice.

"Come here at once. Why have you been out so long?"

"I, um, I met a friend of mine from school down there."

"Oh, yes?" said his father, disbelieving. "In the basement, I suppose?"

"No, of course not. On the stairs."

"Who was it?" asked his mother.

"Andrew."

"I thought you didn't like him."

"Oh, yes, I do," said Tony decisively. "And you know what? He asked me to go and have a game of

Monopoly with him. Can I please take my board down?"

"Now?"

"It's not even seven-thirty," begged Tony. He was thinking of the vampires, who had already been waiting for him for at least five minutes. And if the second vampire *was* Gregory, there would be a terrible fight if he kept them waiting much longer.

"Funny to invite you and then ask *you* to bring the game along," remarked Tony's dad.

"Not really," said Tony. "He doesn't have one."

"Where does this Andrew friend of yours live?" asked his mom.

"On the, um, second floor."

His mother held his gaze searchingly for a minute, then relented. "All right. But by eight, I want you back here in the apartment."

"Absolutely," said Tony, and bit his tongue in an effort not to smile with relief. "See you. . . ."

He tiptoed over to the hook with the keys hanging on it, took off the storeroom key, and slipped it into his pocket. He was already at the front door when his father called after him, "What about the Monopoly board?"

"Oh, yeah," murmured Tony, "of course."

He ran to his room. Where had he last seen the board? On his table? Frantically he rummaged through his drawers. It wasn't on the bookshelf either, and in the closet he could find only stamp albums and comics. Finally, his glance fell on a collection of games in one box. That would have to do. He tucked it under his arm and went out into the hall.

"See you later," he called, and hurried quickly to the elevator.

3 / Coffin Bearers

"At last," the larger vampire greeted him when he finally reached the basement. "You sure took your time about it."

"I had to tell my parents where I was going. I pretended I was on my way to see a friend."

"Hah! Friend!" spat the larger vampire. "Come and help with the coffin."

"What about the game?" said Tony helplessly.

"What game?" The vampire surveyed the box under Tony's arm. "Give it to me." He snatched it away and hid it in the folds of his cape.

"Hey!" protested Tony, looking imploringly at Rudolph. But the young vampire only shrugged his shoulders.

"Now, let's get going," growled the larger vampire. "Take the handles—you in front, Rudolph in back."

"What about you?" asked Tony, lifting the coffin. "I'll hold the door open."

The coffin was heavier than Tony had imagined—and Rudolph was not the strongest of carriers. With aching muscles, they reached the door of the storeroom.

"Well?" The larger vampire grinned, watching Tony and Rudolph rubbing their stinging fingers.

"How in the world did you get it all the way here?"

"Greg carried it," replied Rudolph.

"All by myself, no less," boasted Greg.

"I see," said Tony. So it *was* Gruesome Gregory. He looked at him respectfully. It certainly could be dangerous to get on the wrong side of *him*.

"Aren't you going to unlock the door?" growled Greg.

"Of course," answered Tony, fumbling in his pocket for the key. With trembling hands, he turned the lock and the door creaked open. Greg pushed the coffin inside and shut the door behind them.

"Should—should I turn on the light?" asked Tony, shaking.

"Light?" snorted Greg. "Are you crazy?"

"But you can't see anything."

"I can," declared Greg, and began to push over to one side all the cardboard boxes that stood in the middle of the floor.

"Careful!" cried Tony. "Those are bottles of wine."

But it was too late—there was the tinkle of broken glass, and a large puddle began to form on the floor.

"Big deal," said Greg. "It'll dry out."

"Where should we put my coffin?" Rudolph wanted to know.

"In the back, with all the junk," said Greg.

There was an indignant protest from Rudolph. "Why do I have to be put with the junk?"

"It'll be less noticeable that way," explained Greg.

"B-but we haven't got any junk," said Tony. "Dad cleans the storeroom out once a month."

"That's just great!" said Rudolph. "Now you tell me, Greg, okay? What if he finds me?"

"Tony'll know how to stop him," said Greg, giving Tony an encouraging nudge on the shoulder. "Won't you?"

"Oh, sure," muttered Tony, who was feeling more and more miserable at the thought of what the next weeks would bring. "I—I'll pick up the pieces of bottle." He groped in one of the boxes and let out a cry. "Ow, my finger!"

At once Greg's interest was aroused. "Let me see—is there any blood?" he asked excitedly.

"Yes. I mean no," said Tony, and quickly put his finger in his mouth. It was bleeding pretty badly, but he said, "It's stopped already." Vampires and blood. He already knew that they fed on blood, and he had read somewhere that they could smell a drop of blood several yards away. "Don't you think we should get moving with hiding this coffin?" he suggested. "I have to be getting back. . . ."

"That can wait," said Greg. "First I want to see your finger."

"H-here," stuttered Tony. The cut was still there, but it had stopped bleeding.

Greg sniffed at each finger. "Nothing," he grumbled, turning away in disappointment. "Come on, let's get rid of this thing. I'm hungry."

"Can't I turn the light on now?" asked Tony. If he didn't, who could tell what more damage they might cause?

"Okay," growled Greg.

Tony turned on the light—and stood transfixed, his hair standing on end. Greg was a terrifying sight, white as chalk, with a gaping, scarlet mouth, from the corners of which protruded two long, dangerous-looking teeth—the teeth of a beast of prey.

"What's the matter with you?" asked Greg. "Decided you can't hack it anymore?"

"N-no," answered Tony.

"I'd like it to be behind that chest," Rudolph decided.

"Sorry—you can't," said Tony. "That's got potatoes in it, and it's nailed to the wall."

"Well, next to it, then."

Greg pushed the coffin against the wall and looked

around him. His eyes fell on a stack of wooden planks that Tony's father was going to use to panel the kitchen wall.

"Those are perfect," he announced.

He leaned them up against the wall of the store-room so that the coffin lay hidden behind them. "So, that's that," he said. "Now I must have something to eat before I die of hunger. You coming, Rudolph?"

Tony was on his toes at once, but Greg's hunger pangs didn't seem to be directed at him—he was standing at the window and had already pulled the grating aside. With one powerful leap, he sprang up and clambered through it. Rudolph followed.

"And leave the window open, understand?" hissed Greg, spreading out his arms under his cape.

"Okay," said Tony. He heard the vampires fly off into the darkness; then everything was quiet.

If only it was all just a dream, thought Tony. But there stood the planks against the wall, and behind them was the coffin.

Dejectedly he went to the door, flicked off the light, and pushed the catch down on the lock. The next few weeks were certainly going to cause some problems.

4 / Gloomy Outlook

Tony's parents were still watching television.

"Well, how was it?" called his father.

"Fine," answered Tony, hoping to go on past the living-room door and into his bedroom. He was completely worn out.

"How was the game of Monopoly?"

Tony stopped. "Fine," he said with a yawn.

"Did you bring it back?"

"Yes."

"That's funny," said his father. "I could have sworn you weren't carrying it when you walked past the door."

"I've already put it back in my room."

"I see. In that case, how do you explain that it's sitting here on top of the television?"

That woke Tony up with a start. "Oh. I, um,

couldn't find it before, so I took the collection of games with me instead."

"Where is it?"

"I left it at his apartment by mistake."

Dad snorted with impatience. "Well, isn't that something?" he said. "Really, son, you have to learn to be less careless with your things...."

But at that moment the news began, and at once the man's face assumed a look of total absorption. With an exasperated gesture in Tony's direction, he indicated that the interview was over.

"May I go now?" Tony could hardly keep the anger out of his voice.

His father did not answer, but his mom stood up and put her arm around Tony's shoulders. "Come on," she said, and went out with him. Once in the hall she said, "You know what Dad's like with the News Round-Up."

"He bugs me to death, and then acts like he's got nothing better to do than watch the stupid news!" fumed Tony.

"He just wants to hear what's going on in the world."

"Huh!" snorted Tony. "Every day's the same. There's always a war going on somewhere, and the politicians never change anything. He'd be better off if he paid more attention to what's going on around *him*!"

"Paid attention to what?" asked his mom with a smile.

"For starters, he could notice that I'm feeling neglected, and that he cares more about the news than about us."

"He's not always like that," said Tony's mother soothingly. "He's going to begin paneling the kitchen walls with that wood this weekend."

"What?" cried Tony. "I thought he was going to wait until his vacation."

"He was, but he's decided to start it this weekend."

"I'll—I'll help him, then," said Tony hurriedly. There might still be a chance to keep Dad out of the basement.

"That would be sweet of you. Sleep tight, dear."

"Good night," murmured Tony.

Today is Tuesday, he thought as he lay in bed. That means three more days till Saturday. He'd have to talk to Rudolph tomorrow. Maybe together they'd be able to think of a way out.

5 / Early-Morning Mood

The next day was gray and rainy. It was already beginning to get dark by six o'clock. Tony's father was never home before six-thirty, and Tony's mother was sitting in her room grading papers, a job from which she was "not to be disturbed, even if the house is falling down," she had told Tony.

It was therefore the ideal opportunity to visit Rudolph in the basement without being noticed. Quietly, Tony snuck across the hall, took the key off the hook, and closed the front door behind him.

He took the elevator down to the basement. He didn't meet anyone on the way, and the basement was deserted too. The smell of mold and decay struck his nostrils immediately—he had never noticed it before. Was it Rudolph? He stopped in front of the door marked "Noodleman" and listened.

"Rudolph?" he whispered, and knocked on the door. "It's me, Tony."

No answer. Maybe Rudolph had already gone out? But it was still too light for that. Vampires are not allowed to leave their coffins before sunset.

"Rudolph?" he repeated, a little more loudly.

Again all was silent. Maybe he had never come back to the basement, but had spent the night somewhere else? But no, that wasn't possible either; he had to sleep in his coffin.

Tony knocked again. When there was still no answer, he unlocked the door and went in. By the dim light, he could see that the window was barred. Rudolph must be in his coffin.

Carefully, he inched around the planks of wood and studied the coffin that lay behind them. The lid was closed, and only the funny moldy smell showed it wasn't empty. From inside there came a muffled groan, something bumped and thumped, and then the lid was raised slowly. Rudolph's ashen face emerged. His eyes were still shut, his mouth open in a gigantic yawn that revealed his powerful pointed canine teeth.

"Rudolph?" whispered Tony.

The little vampire gave a start. "Who's there?" he croaked.

"Me," answered Tony.

"Oh, it's only you," said the vampire, sounding

relieved. He stretched. "Something the matter?"

"Yes. I mean no. Dad wants the planks."

The vampire yawned. "Which planks?"

"These, of course," said Tony, pointing to the pieces of wood. "And not only that, he keeps all his tools down here also."

The vampire heaved himself up onto the edge of his coffin and sighed. "What's any of this got to do with me?"

"Don't you see?" Tony's voice sounded too loud. "When he comes down here, he'll find you!"

"Oh." The vampire rubbed his eyes sleepily. "All these problems before I've eaten my breakfast."

"We've got to think of something," Tony urged.

"If only I weren't so tired," whined the little vampire. "I can't think."

"Today is Wednesday," continued Tony anxiously. "He wants to get the wood on Saturday."

The vampire turned his head to the wall and sighed. "I understand," he said, "but I just can't think on an empty stomach . . . and anyway, you've disturbed my morning routine." Now he sounded angry. "I always read for a while before I get up."

He lay back in his coffin with an injured look on his face and felt under his pillow for candles, matches, and a book. Without looking at Tony again, he lit the candle, fixed it securely to the edge of his coffin, and began to read. Tony could not believe his eyes. There was the vampire in the middle of this crisis, calmly lying there reading *The Revenge of Dracula*.

Did he expect Tony to cope with the whole thing by himself? That was really kind of unfair—he had some nerve to think he could lie there while Tony took care of all the little problems and difficulties as they cropped up.

"You haven't got any idea about what friends are for," said Tony angrily.

"Ssssh!" hissed the vampire. "If anyone disturbs my reading, I fly into a terrible rage."

Tony bit his lip with frustration. Now what? He looked around the storeroom and tried to think. Should he put back the planks where they were before? But then what could he use to cover the coffin? Why was their storeroom so neat all the time? Everybody else had tons of junk that they could have easily used to hide Rudolph. What if he threw a large sheet over the coffin? But then Dad would be sure to know what was underneath. No, it wouldn't work. The only way out was to somehow stop Dad from coming down here at all.

"I'm going now," he said.

"Don't come down so early next time" was all he got for an answer. "I'm never at my best first thing in the morning."

"You can say that again!" growled Tony as he left the room.

6 / Lame Excuses

Saturday was the day that Tony liked to sleep late. By the time he woke up at ten or ten-thirty, his parents had usually had breakfast and gone shopping. Tony's bowl would be left on the kitchen table with some cereal in it, and a glass for milk next to it.

But this particular Saturday morning Tony woke up very early. He turned on the light and looked blearily around the room. Wasn't he in the basement, and wasn't Dad about to open the lid of the coffin . . . ? It must have been only a dream, because here he was in bed wearing his pajamas.

He looked at his clock. Seven-fifteen! Even his parents would still be asleep. Tony drew the covers up around his chin with a sigh. He was sure he would not go back to sleep again—he was much too nervous for that. Would his plan work? And what would happen if it didn't?

He took out his newest book, *Voices from the Vault*, and tried to read. But the Horror of the Depths described in the book seemed to him so similar to the horror that was at this moment lying in the depths of his apartment complex that he did not feel like reading about it, and he put the book aside.

Maybe the best thing to do would be to go and make breakfast. He climbed out of bed and went to the bathroom. He studied his reflection in the mirror. He looked pale and ashen—like his parents sometimes did on a Sunday morning, after a particularly late night out. He scrubbed his face with his washcloth until his skin glowed. Then he dressed and went into the kitchen. He filled the coffee maker and put a saucepan of water, to boil some eggs, on the stove.

Next he set the table, and tried to think what else he needed. Of course—how about some doughnuts? He waited till the eggs were ready, then ran down to the corner store and bought a box. Well, he thought, if this doesn't impress Mom and Dad, nothing will. He went over to their bedroom door and knocked.

"Yes?" mumbled his mother sleepily.

"Breakfast!" called Tony. A couple of minutes passed; then his mother appeared in the doorway.

"Have you really made breakfast?"

"Of course," said Tony, as though it were nothing unusual. "Hurry up, or the eggs will get cold."

"Okay, we're coming," she said. "Let me just wake your father up. He should be awake by now anyway, if he's going to get moving on the kitchen."

Tony shuddered. He'd almost forgotten.

"What's all this? Breakfast ready?" asked his father with undisguised astonishment when he saw the kitchen table. He sat down, took his egg out of its eggcup, and shook it.

"Hard as a rock," he teased.

Tony looked hurt. "You don't believe I can even boil an egg!"

"What's the coffee like?" his dad asked his mom.

"Excellent."

"Not incredibly surprising," grumbled Tony. "The machine made it automatically."

"Doughnuts too!" Dad took one and bit into it. "I really wouldn't recognize my own son anymore." After a pause he looked at Tony searchingly. "What's it all for?" he asked, laughing. "Have you been up to something?"

"Me? No, of course not," answered Tony.

"Bad grades on your homework?"

"No."

Dad took another bite of his doughnut without

taking his eyes off Tony. "I just bet something is up," he said.

Tony hesitated. "I—I lost the key to the basement storeroom," he said at last.

"You what?" shouted his father. "How am I supposed to get the wood and the tools?"

"I d-don't know," mumbled Tony, trying his hardest to look ashamed.

"How did you lose it?"

"While I was out on my bike yesterday."

"Didn't you look for it?"

"No," said Tony. "It was already dark."

"Then you'll go and look for it now!" thundered his father. "How can you be so careless?"

"I'll go right away," said Tony.

"Let him at least finish his breakfast in peace," interrupted Tony's mom. "The key's not that important."

"I'm not hungry anymore," said Tony. At the door, he paused. "Are—are you going to begin working anyway?" he asked cautiously.

"How can I without any tools?" growled his father.

On his way down in the elevator, Tony sang as loudly as he could. He was filled with the sweetness of victory. His plan had worked! No one had guessed that the storeroom key was at that very moment safely in his pants pocket. He'd come back with it in the afternoon, but by then it would be too late for Dad to start working. Then this evening his parents were going to the movies—and tomorrow his grandparents were coming for the day, so Dad wouldn't be able to do it then either. Still singing, Tony headed over to his friend Josh's house, where he would play Monopoly until the afternoon—with Josh's board, of course.

7 / A Late Visitor

It was eight-thirty. Tony was lying on his bed listening to music. Not much earlier, his parents had left the apartment in a rush, as always. As usual, Tony had asked, "When will you be back?" and Dad had said, "About midnight, or thereabouts." That suited Tony perfectly. Probably his parents thought that he did not like being left alone. Which was true, except of course when there was a good movie on television. And especially—he turned over and groped for the newspaper listing all the shows—when there was a fantastic horror movie on like tonight, with all his favorite actors in it.

Something knocked on the window. Startled, Tony lifted his head. He had not yet drawn the curtains, and he could make out the shape of a figure on the windowsill. Was it Rudolph? Or his sister Anna? He noticed how fast his heart had begun to beat.

The figure knocked again, and then he heard Rudolph's voice. "Come on! Open up!"

He ran over to the window and opened it. With a single bound, the vampire landed in the room.

"Phew!" he gasped. "She almost got me."

"Who?" asked Tony.

"Aunt Dorothy. She's spying around outside."

"What?" cried Tony. "Does she know I live here?"

"Of course," said the vampire. Then he giggled. "But she doesn't know *I* live here too."

Tony had turned as white as a sheet. "H-how did she find out wh-where I live?"

"She always followed me before I was banned from the vault," explained Rudolph.

Tony stared at him in disbelief. Hadn't the little vampire once said that Aunt Dorothy was the worst of the bunch? Supposing one night she came and tapped on his window and he opened it unsuspectingly . . . ?

"Wh-what does she want?" he stammered.

"To find out where my coffin is." The vampire stared out into the darkness, rubbed his bony fingers, and smiled. "But this time I've outsmarted her."

Tony was still trembling. It was a terrifying thought, that Aunt Dorothy was on the lookout for him.

"Will she come back?" he asked anxiously.

"Not tonight, that's for sure," said the vampire.

"What about tomorrow?"

The vampire shrugged his shoulders. "The main thing is that she doesn't find my coffin."

Tony glared at him in anger. "You're the most self-centered person I've ever met," he shouted.

"I'm not a person," said the vampire haughtily.

"Vampire, then. You're worse than a corpse, that's for sure. Friendship doesn't count for anything with you."

But instead of being ashamed, the vampire looked very pleased with himself. "I wish the others had heard you say that." He smiled. "They're always saying I'm too nice."

Tony turned away angrily. The vampire didn't seem bothered in the slightest by anything apart from his own problems, and even the thought that his bloodthirsty Aunt Dorothy was on Tony's trail didn't seem to disturb him one bit.

"Well, whatever else you are, you're certainly not a friend."

"How can you say that?" exclaimed the vampire. "I came all the way here to take you to a Vampire Ball."

"To a—what?" asked Tony.

"A Vampire Ball." Rudolph proudly opened his cape, and Tony could see he was wearing another underneath. "Or are your parents at home?"

"No," said Tony. "But what *is* a Vampire Ball?"

The vampire waved his hand around. "You'll have to find out for yourself." Then, suddenly businesslike, he added, "Come on. We've got to turn you into a vampire."

Tony almost screamed. He knew only too well from his books how people are turned into vampires. Involuntarily, his hand flew to his neck in protection, but the little vampire just smiled.

"Not like that," he said. "You've got to make yourself up."

"Make myself up?" echoed Tony.

"Of course. Isn't there any baby ointment? Or lipstick?"

"Y-yes. In the bathroom."

"Well, what are we waiting for?"

8 / Tony's New Look

Once in the bathroom, the little vampire helped Tony put on his cape. Then he took a step or two backward and looked him up and down critically. "That's no good. Your jeans are sticking out of the bottom," he declared. "No vampire wears jeans."

"What do you wear?" asked Tony.

The vampire lifted his cape so that Tony could see his black woolly tights. "These," he said. "Hand knitted."

"I don't have any tights," said Tony.

"You don't?" asked the vampire. "What do you wear in the winter?"

"Long underwear," said Tony. "It's white."

"Yuck," exploded the vampire. "I'll tell you what. I'll lend you mine."

"Yours?" Tony was shocked. To have to wear a

vampire's vampirish tights was really the last straw. But the vampire had already started to take them off.

"I've got two pairs on anyway," he said, "because of the holes. . . ." He held the tights out to Tony, who took off his jeans and put them on the stool.

"I hope they're big enough," he muttered, pulling them on with care.

"Should be," said the vampire cheerfully. "They're Greg's."

That's great, thought Tony. Not only do I have to wear these revolting things, but in addition I may get into trouble with Gregory about them. What was more, the wool was terribly itchy.

"Maybe it would be better if I stayed at home," he suggested hesitantly, not wanting the little vampire to guess what he was thinking.

"You don't want to let an opportunity like this slip by, do you?" exclaimed Rudolph.

"N-no," said Tony. "I—it's just, well, how many vampires do you think will be there?"

"All of us. That's why we have to be dead certain we've disguised you properly."

"*Dead* certain? How do you mean?"

"Well, that no one recognizes you and you don't arouse suspicion. Let's start with your hair." He grabbed the brush and tousled Tony's hair with it so roughly that he yelped.

"Ow! Watch out—you're messing up my cape."

"How? Do you have dandruff?" said the little vampire, laughing. "Well, that's great! The cloak looks really good and used. Let's move on to your face now. Where's the baby ointment?"

"In the closet," replied Tony, plucking at his hair, which now stood out from his head like a wild feather duster.

The vampire found the baby ointment and put a generous squirt on Tony's cheeks.

"Now rub it on," he ordered.

"That's easier said than done," grumbled Tony, trying to smear the glutinous white paste more evenly over his face.

"That'll do," said the vampire. "Now we just shake some powder over the top." With that, he seized the talcum powder and shook it liberally all over Tony's face. Poor Tony gasped for air, but the vampire rubbed his hands together delightedly and chortled, "A real little killer! Now, where's the lipstick?"

"In the bottom drawer," said Tony in a strangled voice.

The vampire undid the lipstick and looked at it ecstatically. "Bloodred," he murmured, and held it under his nose and sniffed it. His face darkened immediately, and he hissed with disappointment. "Huh, it's sweet as sugar. Obviously no good to eat."

He began to outline Tony's lips with swift, deft

strokes. "With or without a drop of blood?" he asked.

"What would you advise?"

"With," said the vampire, and made a couple of red dots at the corner of Tony's mouth. "It looks more realistic like that, at any rate for vampire kids. Or did you think our parents ran around after us wiping our mouths?" He giggled at the thought. "So, all that's left are the bags under your eyes."

"More makeup?" asked Tony wretchedly. It was already hot enough under all the ointment and powder.

"Of course. To make you look really dead. What can we use?"

"Eyebrow pencil?" suggested Tony. "There, on the second shelf."

The vampire took the pencil and made deep circles under Tony's eyes. "No one would ever recognize you," he said triumphantly.

"What if it comes off?"

"It won't. Just don't get too close to anyone."

"Don't worry, I won't," said Tony emphatically, thinking of Aunt Dorothy and all the little vampire's other terrifying relations.

"There you are!" The little vampire stepped back, looking pleased. "You can look now."

Tony's knees felt like rubber as he got up from the edge of the bathtub, where he had been sitting, and looked in the mirror. What he saw exceeded his

wildest expectations: A grisly, chalk-white mask stared back at him; the bright red mouth looked like it was dripping with blood; and two eyes looked out furtively from deep-set sockets.

"That's n-not me," he stuttered.

"Pleased?" The vampire grinned happily. "No one will recognize you—not even Anna," he added with a wicked grin.

"So your sister's going to be there?"

"Of course. She's expecting you."

Tony cleared his throat to hide his embarrassment, and changed the subject. "I've had a very hard time trying to keep my dad out of the basement," he said.

"So what?" The little vampire sounded unconcerned.

"I won't be able to keep him away next Saturday. Can't you go back to the vault before then?"

"We'll see," said Rudolph. "Maybe there'll be news."

"I hope so." Tony sighed.

"Now let's go," said the little vampire, moving over to the window.

"I—I don't think I can remember how to fly anymore," said Tony. It had been a while since Rudolph had taught him.

"Can't you?" asked the vampire, giving Tony a friendly dig in the ribs. "Just do what I do. I shut my eyes before I jump—it always helps."

"Are you scared too?" asked Tony in amazement.

"Not anymore," said the vampire, and sprang off the windowsill into the night.

"M-me neither." And Tony shut his eyes—and flew!

9 / The Flight to the Valley of Doom

A gentle wind swelled Tony's cape and ruffled his tousled hair. He spread out his arms and found himself gliding.

"Come on," said Rudolph, tugging at his cape. "The Ball must have started by now." He pumped his arms strongly and climbed higher. Tony had difficulty keeping up.

"Wait for me," he called. "I can't go so fast." He looked down anxiously. The houses looked like toys, and his own room, in which he had left a light burning, was just a tiny bright square.

The vampire slowed down a little. "No stomach for heights?" He grinned.

"Are you kidding?" said Tony quickly, as the moonlight revealed Rudolph's scornful expression.

The vampire looked relieved. "Well, it's a good

thing," he said. "We've got another thirty miles to fly."

"That far!" screamed Tony.

"You didn't think that one hundred vampires could hold a get-together just anyplace?"

"One hundred?" Tony was scared again. "Where do you meet?"

"In the ruins in the Valley of Doom."

"Valley of Doom? Aren't there werewolves there?"

The little vampire smiled. "You don't believe in those fairy tales?"

"Well," Tony defended himself, "I believe in vampires, don't I?"

"What?" spat Rudolph. "You dare lump vampires together with werewolves?"

"No, no," added Tony quickly. "I just meant that most people don't believe in vampires or werewolves either."

"Then they're dumb," pronounced the little vampire scornfully. "Of course there have never been such things as werewolves. They're a vampire invention."

"A vampire invention?"

"Yes. It was the easiest way to keep nosy humans from snooping around our bodies."

Tony looked so amazed that the vampire had to laugh. "Our great-great-great-great-great-grandvampire, Elizabeth the Sweet-Toothed, thought it up. She didn't like humans spying on the Vampire Balls."

"Weren't people frightened of vampires then?"

"Oh, yes. But they knew that vampires never eat or drink during their festivities." Then he grinned. "Vampires get that over and done with before the party starts."

"How bizarre. At a human party, the food and drinks are the most important part of the evening."

The vampire shook his head. "You humans have no idea how to behave," he said.

Tony thought for a moment. "Does that mean that the vampires will have eaten tonight before they all meet at the ruins?"

"Of course."

"I see." Tony let out a great sigh of relief. "I hadn't realized." He was definitely looking forward to the party now! "So what was the werewolf idea?" he asked.

"Simple," said the vampire. "In those days, there were wolves everywhere. Elizabeth the Sweet-Toothed only had to spread the rumor that the wolves that lurked around the ruins were in fact evil men, who turned into ravening beasts after sunset. Soon no one came near the ruins anymore, and the vampires could hold their festivities in peace."

"Are there still wolves around?" asked Tony shyly.

"No," said the vampire, laughing. "But the Valley

of Doom still has a bad reputation. Anyway, the vampires were responsible to a certain extent for the decline in the number of wolves over the years. You see, in times of hardship, famine especially . . ."

Tony felt himself blanch. He didn't like to be reminded of the vampires' grisly eating habits.

"Look!" shouted the vampire. "There it is—the Valley of Doom."

In the pale light of the moon they peered down on a group of shadowy ruins in a clearing, looking dismal and menacing. It was a rambling old building. Only the outside walls of each side wing were still standing. In contrast, the main block looked as if it was in fairly good condition, as far as Tony could see.

"It's so dark," he whispered.

"Vampires don't need much light," answered Rudolph, "but there'll be candles in the main hall."

He flew on purposefully to the main tower, and landed on one of the parapets.

"Here?" Tony was surprised. He had landed next to the vampire and was looking anxiously toward a flight of crumbling steps that led to the inside of the tower.

"We always come in from above," explained the vampire. "At least, almost always." He jumped off the parapet and set off down the steps.

"Wait!" called Tony, knees knocking, and he went clambering down behind him.

45

10 / A Suspicious Reception

At first there was enough moonlight to show Tony where he should put his feet on the crumbling steps, but after the first bend in the stairs it was pitch-dark. Tony felt his way tentatively with his toes, and more than once he had to clutch onto the cold stone wall of the tower or he would have fallen. It seemed to last forever before a feeble glimmer of light appeared on a landing. There stood the little vampire. Tony looked around uneasily. Everything seemed to contribute to the atmosphere of gloom and eeriness: the stairs, rotted and crumbling, which led on deeper in the darkness; the glistening wet walls of the tower with all the strange clefts and crannies, in which hundreds of bats had their homes, he was sure; and the dark passageway leading into the very center of the ruins.

"Hurry up," said Rudolph, taking him by the arm. "We have to keep moving."

"Where?" Tony hesitated.

"To the Great Hall. Can't you hear the music? That's Sabina the Sinister playing the organ."

Rudolph hurried down the hallway, taking Tony with him. By now Tony could hear the organ music too, slow and solemn like in church.

"Is that really Sabina the Sinister?"

"Oh, yes. We vampires love music," said Rudolph enthusiastically.

They came to a large, empty hall with the moonlight shining through its broken windows. Pieces of masonry and broken glass littered the floor.

"We're almost there," whispered Rudolph. His pale face had a look of excitement and his teeth chattered together in a most unnerving manner. An even larger hall opened up before them. Black shrouds were hanging from the windows, and black candles burned in the holders on the walls.

"Here," whispered the vampire, and at once a dark figure slid out from the shadow of the doorway and came over to them. It was a lean-looking vampire, with long scars on his face. It looked at them suspiciously and hissed, "Who are you?"

The little vampire made a bow. "I am Rudolph Sackville-Bagg," he said, "and this"—gesturing toward Tony—"is a friend of mine."

"A friend of yours. Is he a vampire?"

"Of course!"

"He looks human to me."

The hair on Tony's neck prickled.

"He's foreign," explained the little vampire. "He comes from Italy."

"Are there vampires in Italy?"

"Oh, yes. There's a villa there, Matchimo or something, and it's full of them."

"What's the family name?" pursued the lean vampire.

"The family name?" Rudolph hedged. "It's Noodlemaniori the Multitudinous."

"Multitudinous?"

"Yes, there are so many of them, you see."

"What about your friend? What's his name?"

"Antonio Noodlemaniori the Melancholy."

Tony grinned surreptitiously. Antonio Noodlemaniori—it sounded much better than Tony Noodleman, that was for sure.

"I don't know," said the lean vampire indecisively. "I've never heard of . . ." He thought for a moment, then leaned forward and sniffed at Tony's cape. His face brightened for the first time. "Mmmm," he sighed. "Genuine coffin!" He scrutinized Tony once more from head to toe, but in a slightly more friendly way. "All right, then," he growled, "you can go in."

Tony and Rudolph exchanged relieved glances.

Then, just as they were about to enter, the other vampire laid a heavy hand on Tony's shoulder.

"Just a second."

"Y-yes?" said Tony, shaking.

"What's the climate like in Italy?"

Tony was taken aback. "It—it's lovely," he stammered.

"I might come and visit you sometime," said the vampire, letting his hand drop. "My rheumatism never gets any better in all this damp."

With these words he took up his position again in the doorway, and looked cheerfully beyond Rudolph and Tony into the Great Hall.

11 / The Joys of Dancing

Tony stopped on the threshold and held his breath. The smell of decay was so overpowering that for a second he thought he would have to leave. It wasn't only that, either—onions and rotten eggs were also much in evidence. The little vampire took long, deep breaths. "Ah," he sighed. "How lovely it smells!"

Tony cleared his throat. "A drop of fresh air would be nice," he murmured.

"What?" Rudolph snorted. "Fresh air? You'd be deserted by all true vampires." Looking around furtively, he added, "Don't let anyone hear you say things like that. You'll give yourself away. Anyway, there'll be the presentation of the Perfume Prize soon."

"Perfume Prize?" asked Tony.

"The prize for the vampire who smells the most."

Just then the organ music started again, and the vampires, who had been sitting at tables around the room, rose to their feet and made their way in pairs to the middle of the hall.

"Come on, " said Rudolph. "Let's dance too."

"U-us?" faltered Tony.

"Come *on*." The little vampire hooked an arm with Tony's and led him onto the floor, flashing his terrible grin and nodding affably to all sides. "You be the girl," he whispered. "Put your hands on my shoulders, bend your head a little, and gaze at me lovingly."

"M-me?" groaned Tony. "A girl?"

"Of course. That will be the least noticeable. All vampire children look alike."

Tony gulped, but glancing around at the many vampires who were already looking curiously in their direction, he decided that the best thing would be to follow Rudolph's instructions. He sank his head to his shoulder and looked dreamily at his feet, while Rudolph whirled him around in a circle till everything was dancing in front of his eyes.

"I feel dizzy," he moaned, but Rudolph held him all the more firmly.

"You dance like a dream," he breathed.

"Really?" Tony was embarrassed. Dancing was not his favorite occupation.

"Yes," replied Rudolph. "You should see Greg trying to dance."

"What's that about me?" interrupted a hoarse voice. A tall vampire emerged from the throng and came up to them with slow, purposeful strides. It was Gruesome Gregory. Tony blanched. What if he recognized . . . ?

"Nothing," said Rudolph hastily.

"You were talking about me," accused Greg, his voice cracking.

"I just said, 'There's Greg,' " said Rudolph, who couldn't think of a better explanation on the spur of the moment.

"Why?" growled Greg.

"Because . . ." Rudolph looked helplessly at Tony. "My friend here from Italy wanted your autograph."

"My autograph?" Greg surveyed Tony carefully from under lowered lids. "Why mine?"

Rudolph gave an extravagant gesture. "Why do you ask? Your reputation has spread. . . ."

"Really?" Greg was flattered. He signed a patch on Tony's cape, and then quickly turned away and disappeared among the dancers.

"Now my family will know I'm here," muttered Rudolph. "Greg will spread the news."

"Does that matter?"

"We'll have to see. Admittedly, I was banned from the vault—but nobody said anything about dancing!" he finished defiantly, then grabbed Tony around the waist once more and went on with the dance.

12 / The First Kiss

"Tony?" Someone was plucking at his cape, and he spun around, frightened.

"Anna!"

She lowered her eyes shyly. "Greg told me Rudolph was here, and I thought you might be with him. Shall we dance?"

"Um—I'm . . ." He looked helplessly from Anna to her brother. "I've already got a partner."

Anna giggled. "Him?"

Rudolph stepped to one side. "Please—don't let me stop you."

Anna curtsied. "Thank you," she said, then added, "Anyway, I'd make myself scarce if I were you. If Aunt Dorothy sees you . . ."

The little vampire shrugged his shoulders. "So what? This isn't the vault," he said, and turned away.

"Wh-where are you going?" called Tony anxiously, but Rudolph had disappeared. "Thanks for abandoning me!" he muttered.

"You've got me," said Anna, throwing her arms around his neck and drawing close. Tony felt weak and faint.

While they danced, he studied her furtively. She had closed her eyes and was humming softly to the music. Her tiny red lips were smiling, and her cheeks were slightly pink, as if she was really alive. Only her tattered cape reminded him that she was a vampire. But did she count as one? After all, she didn't have vampire fangs yet—they were just beginning to grow on the young vampire. She opened her eyes suddenly. "Nice, isn't it?" she whispered.

"Y-yes," mumbled Tony.

"What do you think of me?"

"Oh." He gulped. "I think you're, um, sweet."

"Really?" Her blush deepened. "Oh, Tony." She stood on tiptoe and kissed him on the lips.

Tony stood rooted to the spot. It seemed to him as though every vampire in the room must be staring at them. He couldn't believe that they were all dancing on as though nothing had happened.

"Are you mad at me?" asked Anna cautiously after a while.

"No," said Tony, embarrassed.

She gave a sigh of relief. "I'm so impetuous, you

know," she explained. "Rudolph says I must learn to master my feelings better—slightly difficult, especially since I could only just 'mistress' them!" she added mischievously.

While she was speaking, Tony licked his lips. They felt dry and smooth, and there was certainly no trace of blood.

"How are you enjoying the party?" asked Anna.

Tony looked around uncertainly. "It's kind of dull, I think."

"I agree. I wanted to put a disco in the dungeon, but the grown-ups wouldn't allow it." She looked up at the organ and made a face. "It's always this oom-pah-pah," she complained.

"We could always go outside for a breath of fresh air," suggested Tony, whose head was reeling.

"Oh, yes!" said Anna enthusiastically. "Let's go for a walk in the moonlight." She took Tony's hand and drew him toward the doorway.

The two of them crossed the hall and reached a dark stairway. The great door stood ajar, and they went through it out into an overgrown garden. The grass was knee-high, and shrubs and bushes had long since grown over the paths. Anna took Tony's hand and laid her head on his shoulder.

"My—my leg's fallen asleep," said Tony loudly, who was finding Anna's increasing friendliness more and more alarming.

56

"I love moonlit nights," said Anna dreamily. Then, in a slightly louder voice, she continued, "Do you see the moon up there? We see only half of it, yet it's really round and beautiful. Many things are probably like that—we ridicule them naively because our eyes don't see them."

Tony glanced at her in surprise. "Did you make that up?" he asked.

"No," she said. "It's from a bedtime song my mother used to sing to me. It's beautiful, isn't it? Moonlight always makes me sentimental." She looked up at Tony with swimming eyes, and a tear rolled slowly down one cheek.

"Wh-why are you crying?" asked Tony.

"Because I'm so happy," she whispered, and ran away.

"Anna!" called Tony in dismay.

This time a voice answered, "Here I am!" Was that Anna's voice? It sounded sort of muffled. A terrible dread came over him. He stood still, holding his breath.

"Where are you?" called the voice, and this time there was no doubt about it: It definitely was not Anna. Who could it be?

Something was gleaming among the bushes. Tony felt himself inexplicably drawn toward it, and nothing he could do could stop him from taking one, then two faltering steps in its direction. Then suddenly something grabbed him from behind.

"Tony!" A voice was calling him urgently. It was Anna. "Quickly! Back to the hall. It's Aunt Dorothy over there. . . ."

Tony glimpsed a shadow emerging from the bushes and hurrying closer and closer, but by then he and Anna had reached the door and closed it tightly behind them. Shaking from head to toe, Anna leaned against it. "She almost got you," she whispered. "And it would have been all my fault."

"I thought she was inside," said Tony.

"I thought so too," said Anna quietly. Her lips quivered, and her face was as white as chalk. "Tony, you must never go outside alone in the moonlight again."

"Don't worry, I won't," Tony assured her.

"Should we go back to the hall?"

"What about Aunt Dorothy?"

"She can't do anything indoors," said Anna. "That's why she wanted to fortify herself first."

"You call that fortifying herself?" said Tony angrily, gingerly feeling his neck.

Anna laughed. "Come on. Maybe they'll be giving the Perfume Prize soon."

13 / Who Has the Best Smell?

The organ music had stopped by the time the two
friends had reached the Great Hall. The vampires
had returned to their tables, and all eyes were staring
fixedly at a small, rather bowed vampire who was
standing in the middle of the hall on a podium.
"Elizabeth the Sweet-Toothed," whispered Anna,
who had found two spare seats near the entrance.

Unlike most other vampires, who seemed to pay
little attention to their appearance, Elizabeth the
Sweet-Toothed was very scrupulously dressed. She
was wearing a spotless cape of black silk, her gray
hair was curled in tiny ringlets, and rings sparkled on
her gnarled old fingers.

"My dear friends," she began. "It gives me great
pleasure that you are all here tonight. The moment

you have all been waiting for has now arrived—the judging of the Perfume Prize. The judges this time are Magdalene the Double-Dealing, Good-Natured Gordon, and Mabel the Mean. I call upon the judges to take their seats."

The three vampires joined her on the podium.

"The one with the glasses is Magdalene," whispered Anna. "She thinks she's got the best legs of any vampire."

"Really?" Tony giggled. Magdalene's cape ended at her knees, and from underneath protruded two short, stocky calves that were anything but elegant.

"Why is that one called Good-Natured Gordon?" asked Tony.

"Can't you see how thin he is? He's so good-natured that he always lets other vampires go first."

Mabel the Mean was taller than the other two vampires by a head. She was in pretty good shape for a vampire, thought Tony, but jealousy and greed had etched deep lines into her face.

"I now ask any vampires who wish to enter this competition to step forward and form a line," called out Elizabeth the Sweet-Toothed. At once about ten vampires left their seats.

"Would the first competitor please come forward."

A thick-set vampire with a completely round bald head stepped onto the podium. "I am George the

Boisterous," he said in a grating voice. "I have entered this competition because to my mind I smell truly spicy."

"Let me smell you," trilled Magdalene the Double-Dealing, and she began to sniff at him. The other two

62

vampires followed suit. Then all three looked at one another and nodded.

"Next!" called Elizabeth the Sweet-Toothed.

This was a tall, lanky vampire. "I am Hannah the Hasty," she said in a high falsetto voice. "My specialty is the fragrance of fresh horse manure."

The judges all snuffled their way around her. Then came a bloated vampire with a double chin and little piggy eyes, a hollow-cheeked girl vampire, a vampire with a patch over one eye, and an ancient vampire who could speak only in a whisper because all but his canine teeth were missing.

Then a tall, broad-shouldered vampire stepped onto the podium. "My name is Gruesome Gregory," he announced. "I am famous for my aroma of decay."

Anna clapped her hand over her mouth. "Greg doesn't have an aroma," she murmured. "It's more like a stink."

With an air of already having won the competition, Gregory strutted about the podium and allowed himself to be sniffed.

"He's in love with himself," said Anna.

After Gregory, two more vampires introduced themselves to the judges and the general gathering, and then the competition was over. Sabina the Sinister sat down at the organ again and played, while the judges went into a huddle with Elizabeth the Sweet-Toothed to come to a decision.

"Do you think Greg will win?" whispered Tony.

Anna shook her head. "Never. I was sitting next to Hannah the Hasty earlier, and Greg's got nothing on her. And who knows what the others smell like?"

At last Elizabeth the Sweet-Toothed raised her arm, and abruptly the music stopped. "My friends," she announced in a stirring voice. "The winner of tonight's competition, the vampire who smells the best, is—" She paused and looked down the row of waiting candidates. "George the Boisterous!"

Thunderous applause broke out. George the Boisterous hobbled over to the podium and bowed.

"The prize is a cuddly blanket for your coffin," announced Elizabeth the Sweet-Toothed, handing over a piece of black cloth.

"Now Greg will be mad," said Anna.

"But it was totally fair," said Tony.

"Greg always thinks it's unfair when he doesn't win," explained Anna, "and it would be better if we didn't get near him. Let's go."

"What about Rudolph?" asked Tony.

"He left already by himself."

14 / Flying Home

"What if Aunt Dorothy catches me?" asked Tony as they stepped onto the top platform of the tower.

"Oh," said Anna, shrugging carelessly, "she's still lurking down there in the garden." She soared up into the air, and Tony spread his arms under his cape and followed her.

"Ah, fresh air," he said, and drew in deep breaths of it.

"What about my Fragrant Earth?" asked Anna peevishly. "Can't you smell my perfume?"

"Yes, of course." There was a certain unpleasant smell, to be sure, but it didn't bother him out here in the open.

"I sprayed on an extra lot tonight, just for you," she declared.

"How considerate."

"Do you really have to go home?" she asked, gazing at Tony with adoring eyes. "We could do something else. I've always wanted to go to a disco, for instance."

"Discos are boring. They're a waste of money."

"We could go swimming, then. A moonlight swim would be very romantic."

"Um—I don't have my bathing suit with me," Tony excused himself quickly.

"So what? Neither do I."

"I've, um, got a cold," said Tony, and sneezed to prove it.

"Huh!" grumbled Anna. "You just don't want to go swimming."

"My parents will be home soon," said Tony. "We've got to get back."

"Okay," said Anna sadly.

For a while they flew on in silence. Tony was angry with himself. He always seemed to mess everything up.

"Want to hear a joke?" he asked finally.

"If you want," replied Anna.

"Fred wanted to buy his dad a shirt for his birthday. 'I'd like a good-looking shirt, please,' he says to the salesman. 'Like the one I'm wearing, sir?' asks the salesman. 'No,' answers Fred, 'a clean one!' "

"Ha, ha," said Anna without smiling.

At least she's said *something*, thought Tony. Fever-

66

ishly, he tried to remember another joke he could tell her. "There's this dog, a boxer, going for a walk down the street. Above him, two floors up, there's a German shepherd on a balcony. 'Jump down here,' calls the boxer. 'We could go for a walk together.' 'Do you think I'm crazy?' answers the German shepherd. 'Do you think I want to end up with a nose like yours?' "

Anna could not stop herself from smiling, but she still stared stonily in front of her.

"Do you know the one about the dachshund?" Tony continued. "A man goes to the movies with his dachshund. The dog laughs and laughs and won't stop. A lady turns around and comments, 'That's a remarkable dog you have there.' 'Yes,' replies the man, 'I think he's unusual too. Would you believe it, when I read the book of this movie to him, he didn't laugh at all!' "

This time Anna laughed softly. The ice was broken. Tony just had to make her laugh out loud now, and he knew exactly the joke to do it.

"Two cows were grazing peacefully in a meadow. Suddenly one of them begins to shiver violently. 'Are you sick?' asks the other one anxiously. 'Oh, no,' her friend replies, 'but here comes the milkmaid with the freezing-cold hands!' "

This was too much for Anna, and she burst out laughing. Tony laughed too, and together they flew on, giggling themselves silly.

"I can't wait to tell Greg that one," she said.

Tony looked flattered.

"Do you know any more?"

Tony shook his head.

"I only know one," said Anna. "A woman goes to her doctor. 'Doctor,' she complains, 'every time I drink a cup of coffee, I get this terrible pain in my right eye.' 'I suggest you take the spoon out of the cup!' advises the doctor."

"My stomach aches from all this laughing," gasped Tony.

"Not so loud," warned Anna. "We've almost reached town."

Just in front of them, the first houses were rising up in the darkness. Tony remembered he had something important to discuss with Anna.

"How long is Rudolph banned from the vault?"

She shrugged her shoulders. "A few weeks. Whatever the family council decides."

"A few weeks!" cried Tony. That was awful. How was he supposed to keep his parents out of the basement for that long? "He leaves everything to me," he complained. "Right this minute, he's lazing in his coffin, reading vampire stories and expecting me to solve all the problems."

"Typical Rudolph," said Anna, grinning. "But you're the one to blame for letting him use you."

"What can I do?" asked Tony. "Just wait and see what happens when my dad finds him?"

"Of course not," Anna replied, "but you have to make it clear to him that he can't stay in your basement forever. The family council meets again next week, and if you're very lucky, maybe the ban will be lifted. In any case, I'll put in a good word for him."

"Are you on the family council?" asked Tony, surprised.

"Of course. You didn't think I'd let anyone else look after my interests?"

By now they had reached Tony's house. His desk lamp was still on in his room. Tony gave a sigh of relief—that meant his parents weren't home yet.

He landed on the windowsill and opened the window.

"Good night, Anna," he said.

"Good night, Tony," she replied. "Don't forget to take off your makeup."

15 / Chicken Fricassee

When Tony woke up the next morning, he was suffering from a terrible headache, and when he tried to get out of bed, everything went black. He sat back on his bed and thought. Had he eaten or drunk anything the day before that could have disagreed with him? But he had not touched anything at the Vampire Ball, and all the food at home was perfectly fine.

Maybe he just hadn't slept long enough? He looked at the clock. Eleven already! He must have had nearly eleven hours of sleep. Maybe the events of last night had just been too much for him, or the smell in the Great Hall had gone to his head.

A gentle tap on the door aroused him. "Tony, are you awake?" asked his mother.

"No," he said, and quickly pulled the covers over his head. He heard his bedroom door being opened, and then felt two hands under the sheet, tickling him.

"No!" he pleaded. "Stop!"

"Are you awake now?" asked his mother, sitting down on the edge of the bed and watching her son emerge from underneath.

"What a sight you are," she said, and gasped in horror.

"What do you mean?" asked Tony.

"Your eyes are all glued up, and your skin's covered with stripes."

"Is it?" mumbled Tony. Maybe he hadn't cleaned himself carefully enough last night. His eyes had refused to stay open any longer as he stood in front of the bathroom mirror, so he had settled for a couple of wipes across his face with a wet washcloth. He hadn't realized the stuff was so difficult to get off. . . .

"Get yourself washed as quickly as you can," ordered his mother. "Grandma and Grandpa are coming for lunch at twelve."

"Oh, yeah," he said, remembering.

"What's for lunch?" he asked his father on the way to the bathroom.

"Your favorite: chicken fricassee."

"And for dessert?"

"Homemade vanilla ice cream."

"Mmmm," said Tony, licking his lips. They still tasted of lipstick.

Just before noon the doorbell rang. Tony had washed and dressed—though not in his good black trousers, despite his mother's protests. "You know what Grandma thinks. . . ." she had said, but Tony had remained obstinate and had put on his jeans. Rudolph's stinking cape and holey tights had been stuffed into a pillowcase and thrown into the very back of his closet.

Tony's grandmother was a round little woman. When she laughed, she revealed a set of perfectly even, pearly-white teeth. Tony had always been very impressed by her teeth—until the time he had gone to spend the night with his grandparents, and had discovered the teeth in a cup the next morning.

Tony's grandfather was not much taller. Usually he wore corduroy pants and a checked shirt, but today he had put on his best suit.

He unwrapped a bunch of tulips and held them out to Tony's mother. And as usual, he pressed a flat little package into Tony's hand—a thick bar of milk chocolate with hazelnuts.

"Not till after you've had your lunch," warned his grandmother.

"Of course not," said Tony.

His grandparents hung up their coats and then sat down at the table in the living room.

"Tony's looking so healthy with those glowing cheeks," remarked his grandmother.

Tony grinned. Not surprising, if she only knew how hard he'd been scrubbing his face with the washcloth.

"But you're still wearing those dreadful jeans," she scolded. "Can't you wear a decent pair of pants, at least on Sundays?"

"Oh, Grandma, everyone wears jeans."

"Grandpa doesn't," she retorted.

"What can I get you, Mother?" offered Tony's dad.

"I'll have a leg, please," she said.

"Tell me," said Tony's grandfather, "have you started fixing up the kitchen yet?"

Tony's father, whose mouth was full of rice, could only shake his head. "Your grandson lost the key to the storeroom door."

"You didn't! How could you lose a thing like that?"

"I did find it again," growled Tony.

"Don't speak with your mouth full," his grandmother scolded.

"What will you do now?" asked Tony's grandfather. "When will you start?"

"I've got to go to a conference all next weekend, and the weekend after that I think I'll need to relax a little."

"Really?" Tony could not believe his ears. This was fantastic. But his relief was short-lived.

"I know what," said Tony's grandfather. "Why not

take a day off this coming week, and I'll come and give you a hand. What do you think of that?"

Tony's father looked surprised. "Not a bad idea," he said. "Tony's not much help at jobs like this," he added.

"What are you talking about?" said Tony indignantly. "I can bring the wood and the tools up from the basement."

"I'd rather do that myself," said Tony's dad. "Or Grandpa could do it. Does Thursday seem okay?"

"Fine," said the old man, nodding.

"That's settled, then." Everyone looked pleased—except for Tony.

"Eat up, Tony," said his grandmother, who had noticed how pale he had become. "This will make you big and strong."

"I know," muttered Tony, stirring his rice around on his plate. His appetite had strangely disappeared.

16 / Waiting for Dusk

"Aren't you going to gymnastics today?" Tony's mother asked on Monday afternoon, just before five o'clock.

"Yes, but it's later. Not until six."

"Why?"

"Why?" Tony hadn't thought up an excuse yet. "I think the teacher had to go to the dentist," he said quickly.

"How strange, when he's supposed to be instructing all of you." Tony's mother shook her head in disgust. "That means it'll be dark when you come home."

"That doesn't matter," said Tony. "Josh will be coming back with me."

"Oh, all right then." She went back to correcting some math homework.

Tony went to his room and read a book till just before six. Then he took his sport bag out of the closet, emptied all of Rudolph's things out of the pillowcase, and stuffed them in with his gymnastics clothes.

Of course he wasn't going to gymnastics tonight. That always happened between five and six o'clock. Tonight he was going to be with Josh from six until quarter to seven, and then, as soon as it was dark, he would sneak downstairs and visit the little vampire in the basement.

"When are you coming back?" asked Tony's mother, as he said good-bye.

"A little after seven," he answered.

On the way back from Josh's house, Tony came, to his horror, face to face with Mrs. Tatum, a neighbor from the fourth floor who was known to all the children in the building as Mrs. Tattle-Tale. As usual, she was wearing her hideous old housedress, and on her head was a transparent nylon scarf that held together a mass of hair curlers.

"Well, well, if it isn't Tony," she said, smiling ingratiatingly. "Running around so late? It's remarkable you're not afraid, all by yourself down here in this dark basement."

"No," muttered Tony, trying to get past her.

But she took his arm in a tight grip and snarled, "Have you noticed how it's begun to stink in here lately? We shouldn't put up with it!"

She paused, and gulped for breath. "If it doesn't get any better, everyone'll have to open up their storerooms so we can find out where the odor's coming from."

Tony was dismayed. "C-can you make people do that?" he stuttered.

"Of course I can!" she said. "Especially in times

like this. . . ." With these words, she let go of his arm and stalked off up the stairs. "Stinks like a pigsty down there," Tony heard her grumble.

He waited in the hallway till all was quiet. Then he crossed over to their storeroom door, knocked, and went in.

The smell of mold and decay certainly did seem more noticeable now—or was it simply that Mrs. Tatum had drawn his attention to it?

He waited by the door and blinked. "Rudolph?" he called quietly. "I brought your things back."

"Why did you come so early again?" was the only answer from the depths of the storeroom.

"Can I turn on the light?" asked Tony cautiously.

"No!" cried the little vampire. "For Lucifer's sake, no electric light so soon after waking me up."

A match flared up brightly, and Tony saw the little vampire light the candle by his coffin.

"I haven't brushed my teeth yet," he said, and pulled a red toothbrush with twisted bristles out of his coffin.

"But you don't have any water," remarked Tony.

"So?" said the little vampire, spitting. "Why would I need water just to brush my gums?"

Tony took the cape and tights out of the sports bag and put them on the edge of the coffin. The vampire didn't seem to want to pay any attention, either to him or to the clothes.

"Why are you mad?" asked Tony finally. "Is it because of the Vampire Ball?"

"Yes."

Tony thought for a moment. "Because I danced with Anna?"

"No!" Although he had been fairly guarded up till that moment, the vampire now boiled. "Because you just ran off, and I was looking all over the ruins for you and ran right into Aunt Dorothy's waiting arms."

"Oh" was all Tony could think of to say. He could certainly understand Rudolph's fright. "What happened?"

"She called Elizabeth the Sweet-Toothed, who is our Vampire-in-chief, and she gave me a punishment, because she said I had some nerve to come to the Vampire Ball when I have been banned from the vault. I didn't know that meant I'd been banned from the party also," he grumbled.

"Does that mean the ban from the vault hasn't been lifted?" asked Tony.

"Not only that—I've also been forbidden to fly for four days."

"What does that mean?" asked Tony, mystified.

"Well, um, that I have to catch my food on foot."

"All I hear is forbidden to do this, forbidden to do that!" said Tony. "Forbidden to go to the vault, forbidden to go to the party, forbidden to fly . . . it's dictatorship!"

The little vampire shrugged his shoulders. "What can I do about it?" he asked.

"Revolt!" said Tony.

But the little vampire only shook his head wearily. "That might work with you humans, but with vampires it would lead to the severest of consequences." His voice lowered. "I'd be forbidden to go on as a vampire."

Tony still did not quite understand.

"That would mean starving to death," said the vampire in sepulchral tones.

Tony was speechless. The vampires seemed to have the most outrageous ways of bringing up their children. He could just be glad he wasn't one. "Can I help in any way?" he asked sympathetically.

The little vampire's eyes began to gleam. "Would you really do that for me?" he asked, licking his lips.

Tony's heart almost stopped beating. "I—I didn't mean like that," he stammered. "I—I meant in some other way."

Rudolph's face fell. "How?" he grunted. "Do you want to help me catch mice?"

"No," said Tony quickly. He really did seem to have a knack for getting himself into hot water.

"I think I'd better get going," said the vampire gloomily. "Who knows how long it's going to take me to get supper tonight." He blew out the candle and stood up.

"Good luck," said Tony quietly. He suddenly felt very sorry for the vampire. He, Tony, could just go upstairs and get a piece of cheese out of the refrigerator whenever he felt hungry.

"Thanks," said Rudolph tonelessly, climbing out the window. "I'm going to need it."

As Tony shut the storeroom door behind him, it occurred to him that he hadn't mentioned what was happening on Thursday. But it was probably just as well he had spared the little vampire this bad news on top of everything else. And anyway, there were still two more days to go. . . .

17 / Uproar in the Hallway

Tony came home on Tuesday happily humming his favorite song, "On top of spaghetti, all covered with cheese. . . ." They had gotten their spelling tests back in school, and Tony, who usually made a lot of mistakes, had gotten only one wrong. That meant he would be given a book as a reward, and he already knew which one he would choose: *Vampire Tales for Advanced Readers.*

He swung the heavy entrance door open and went over to the elevator. Then something made him stop still in his tracks—a shrill woman's voice and the excited yapping of a dog echoed up from the basement. Did it have anything to do with Rudolph, he wondered. He went over to the top of the stairs and listened.

"This must be it!" shrilled the woman's voice.

"This one here. Just look at how my Sudsie's fur's standing on end!"

Then came a man's voice. "That's Noodleman's storeroom."

"Noodleman?" echoed the woman. "I caught their no-good son prowling around here last night with a big bag. He was pretty sneaky when I asked him where he was going. He turned red as a beet."

What lies! thought Tony.

"What time was that?" asked the man.

"Must have been about seven. I thought to myself then there was something fishy going on."

"And since then you've noticed this—uh—strange smell?"

"Oh, no. *That's* been here for almost a week now."

Suddenly there was a series of wild barks, and the woman squealed triumphantly. "There you are! Look at my Sudsie. She thinks there's something funny going on too."

At that moment the entrance door opened and Tony's mother walked in. "What are you doing down here?" she asked in astonishment. "Why aren't you upstairs?"

"Is that you, Mrs. Noodleman?" called the woman's voice from downstairs.

"Yes. What is it?" replied Tony's mother.

"Would you mind coming down here for a minute?" asked the man's voice.

"What's all this about?" Tony's mother asked in a whisper.

"Who knows?" said Tony, shrugging. He wasn't feeling very well at all. He just hoped his mother didn't have the storeroom key with her.

They went down the stairs. A dachshund with a stomach that dragged on the ground came waddling over to meet them, barking furiously. It was Mrs. Tatum's overfed pet, Sudsie.

"I'm glad to see you've brought that good-for-nothing son of yours with you," Mrs. Tatum said in greeting. She had lost her nylon scarf in all the excitement, and her rollers hung half undone around her head.

"Did you call my son a good-for-nothing?" said Tony's mother in surprise.

"Only good-for-nothings sneak around in the basement at seven o'clock at night carrying big bags, if you ask me," countered Mrs. Tatum.

Tony's mother shot him a look that plainly said, "I'll have a word with you about this later," and then said, "I don't agree that you have the right to call my son names. I could call you a few, if it came to that— you gossiping old bag!"

"What did you say?" snorted Mrs. Tatum. "Gossiping old bag, am I? You, you . . ." and she searched for a suitable name to fling back.

"You must have misunderstood what I said," said

Tony's mother coolly. "I said 'one would never call you a gossiping old bag.' "

Mrs. Tatum was speechless.

The superintendent, who up till then had been standing silently next to Mrs. Tatum, now took the opportunity to enter into the conversation. "Mrs. Tatum has been complaining to me about the smell in the basement."

"And what has that got to do with me?" asked Tony's mother.

"She claims it's coming from your storeroom."

"From *our* storeroom?" exclaimed Tony's mother. "That's completely impossible. We clean ours out every four weeks. I've heard some incredible nonsense from you in my time, Mrs. Tatum, but this is really too much."

Mrs. Tatum had paled. "What about my Sudsie?" she asked in a small voice. "Why is she getting all worked up in front of your storeroom, then?"

"How should I know?" Mrs. Noodleman threw a look at the dog. "Some dogs are always yapping at something."

Tony felt as though a weight had dropped from his shoulders. How great that his mom had stood up for him! Of course, she'd want to know what he'd been doing in the basement, but by then he'd have a good excuse.

The wind had been completely taken out of Mrs.

Tatum's sails, and even the super seemed to find the whole business embarrassing.

"Please accept my apologies," he said to Tony's mother, "but you must understand, I have to follow up on complaints of this nature."

Mrs. Tatum swept her dachshund up in her arms and, without another word, she stalked off up the stairs.

"Come on, Tony," said his mother. "I bet you haven't had a snack yet."

18 / Happiness Is a Plate of Spaghetti

"Now then," said Tony's mother after she had sat Tony down at the kitchen table with an unusually great snack—a plate of steaming spaghetti. "What were you up to in the basement at seven o'clock yesterday evening?"

With great concentration, Tony wove two strands of spaghetti onto his fork. "It's a secret," he said.

"Is it also a secret why you skipped gymnastics yesterday?"

Tony looked up with a start. How had she found that out?

"Yes, look surprised!" said Mrs. Noodleman. "I happened to meet Josh's mother, who told me you'd been playing Monopoly with Josh yesterday evening."

"Um, yeah . . . well, you see, I didn't feel like going

to gymnastics yesterday. All that running around in circles, balancing on those beams . . ."

"But you always used to enjoy it so much."

She was right.

"What about Josh? Didn't he feel like it either?"

Tony thought for a moment. She probably knew the truth already, so he said, "Josh quit months ago."

"So you were making all that up about your teacher who had to go to the dentist?" His mother didn't sound *too* mad. In fact, she sounded like she was teasing. "I would simply like to have an explanation for all this haunting of the basement."

"Haunting? You shouldn't joke about things like that," said Tony.

"Well, what *were* you doing in the cellar?"

Tony shook his head. "It's a secret," he repeated.

"I'm so curious," said his mom. "Couldn't you just tell me?"

"You'll find out on Thursday."

"Do I have to wait that long?"

It seemed like she was treating the whole thing as a joke, which was of course the best thing that could happen. As long as she didn't get suspicious, Rudolph was pretty safe, anyway. But Thursday he would have to be out of the basement for good, and Tony would be able to tell his mother that they had had a vampire down there as a guest for a whole week. Tony had to laugh when he thought of what his parents would say when he told them. And he looked forward to the time when he could stop telling these dumb made-up stories.

"Eating spaghetti seems to make you laugh," remarked his mother.

"Happiness is a plate of spaghetti," Tony replied. "Didn't you know?"

After his snack Tony went to his room and sat down at the desk. He opened his notebook and began his grammar homework: What is a gerund? Compose ten sentences, employing a gerund in each. But his thoughts kept returning to Rudolph in the basement, till finally he closed the notebook with a snap. Whatever else happened, he had to talk to Rudolph today and make it clear to him that he couldn't stay in the basement any longer.

But what reason could he give his parents for going down to the basement again this evening? What if he went down at around six, waited for Rudolph to wake up, and then just came up late for supper? Anyone can be held up, can't they?

He opened his notebook once more. Even if he didn't know what a gerund was, he was definitely a master at making up excuses.

19 / An Empty Stomach

"I'm just going out for a few minutes," Tony said a little before six.

"Okay," said his mother, "but don't forget, supper's at seven."

Once downstairs, Tony took out his bicycle. He had to wait awhile, but he'd pass the time somehow. He had brought *Voice from the Vault* with him, so he could at least read if he found a good place to sit and it was still light.

He was back at the building by seven. Quietly, he opened the entrance door. There was nobody around, so he quickly picked up his bicycle and dragged it down the steps to the basement. The hallway was empty, and apart from the moldy smell, which seemed to have grown stronger, everything was the same as usual. He leaned his bike up against a wall and opened the door to the storeroom.

The little vampire was already awake. He was sitting up in his coffin, and by the light of a candle, he studied Tony with huge, hungry eyes. Then he recognized who it was, and the expression on his face turned to one of disappointment.

"Oh, it's you," he said tonelessly.

His hair stood out wildly from his head, and his teeth were clattering furiously, as if he was shivering from extreme cold.

"Rudolph!" shrieked Tony in a shocked voice. "Are you sick?"

"Sick?" echoed the vampire, and tried to laugh. "I'm only about to die of hunger."

"Weren't you able to—catch anything?"

The moan that Rudolph gave as an answer made Tony's hair stand on end. "Not even a mouse!" he groaned, and pressed his hands to his stomach. "If you only knew how empty I feel." He gazed at Tony with gleaming eyes, and ran his tongue slowly over his lips. Tony shivered—it suddenly occurred to him that Rudolph's eyes were fixed on his neck.

"Y-you wouldn't . . ." he began, and took a step backward. Who could say what a starving vampire might or might not do.

But Rudolph shook his head and groaned even more loudly.

"You can walk, I hope?" asked Tony sympathetically.

Rudolph got up and took a couple of shaky steps, then fell back into his coffin. "If only I wasn't so dizzy," he sobbed.

He looked so pathetic that Tony really did feel sorry for him. Was it fair to burden Rudolph with additional worries right now? He should have something to eat first. As always when he thought of what Rudolph liked to eat, a shiver ran down his spine. But he ignored it bravely and said, "Maybe I could help you."

"How?" asked the vampire.

Tony hesitated. "I'm not too bad at catching rabbits," he offered.

"You aren't?" The vampire's face brightened. "Well, we could give it a whirl."

Immediately, he jumped out of the coffin and went to the window. The prospect of food had made him feel much better. Tony began to regret that he had offered to help.

"Um, Rudolph," he said. "About the basement— you see, Dad—and Grandpa . . ."

But the vampire had already opened the window and clambered outside. "Come on," he called. "There are two rabbits!"

20 / Bad Luck

Tony followed him unhappily. Whenever it was a question of his, Tony's, interests, Rudolph always seemed to suddenly become deaf.

Now he was squatting on the lawn and looking around searchingly. "There *were* two here," he whispered.

"I think we should move," said Tony, anxiously looking up at the lighted windows of the apartments above. "Otherwise my parents might see us."

"Where should we go?" asked the little vampire excitedly.

"Over there," said Tony, pointing to the playground that was shielded from inquisitive eyes by tall bushes.

"Are there rabbits over there?" asked Rudolph, his voice filled with doubt.

"Lots," said Tony, although in fact he was not sure. The two of them crept cautiously across the lawn. Tony didn't relax until they were hidden in the bushes.

"So where are the rabbits?" asked Rudolph, looking unenthusiastically at the prickly thorns now surrounding them.

Tony pushed a couple of branches to one side. "There!" he said. "That's their favorite place."

"Is it?" asked the vampire. His voice had become rougher, and his eyes gleamed brightly. With a single bound he vanished between the bushes, but was back almost immediately. His face was scratched and his cape was even more torn. "You call these rabbits?" he asked, holding out two fat spiders for Tony to see.

"Yuck!" exclaimed Tony. He couldn't stand spiders. He turned away quickly, because he didn't relish seeing how vampires tear spiders limb from limb.

But Rudolph plucked at his sleeve. "You don't think I eat spiders?" he asked, and with a look of distaste, he let them drop to the ground. "You've been watching too many bad vampire movies."

"I was just thinking . . ." murmured Tony. Then suddenly he had an idea. "I know! I could go to the hospital for you."

"The hospital?" Rudolph was not impressed.

"They keep blood in jars there, I think."

But the vampire would have nothing to do with it. "I don't eat preserved food," he said.

"I didn't know that." Tony felt hurt.

At that moment they heard footsteps approaching across the playground. At once Rudolph's expression changed. "A human," he whispered, and smacked his lips in anticipation.

Tony jumped. Surely Rudolph wouldn't really try to . . . "I th-thought we were after r-rabbits," he stammered. "A-and if you tr-try to catch anything else . . ."

"What?" scowled the vampire.

"I'll—it'd be betrayal!"

The footsteps were now level with where they lay hidden. Rudolph had bared his needle-sharp teeth and was staring into the darkness of the bushes. His whole body quivered with excitement.

"No," implored Tony.

The vampire turned on him in anger. "Just you keep out of my business," he hissed.

"I-if you try anything," pleaded Tony, "I—I won't be friends with you anymore."

The footsteps faded into the distance. A door opened and closed, then all was still. With a cry, Rudolph clapped his hand to his mouth. "What an opportunity," he wailed. "I won't get one like that again." Gnashing his teeth, he turned on Tony. "You call that helping? I'm starving, *really* starving. I'm

95

going to do this hunting on my own." He pulled his cape around him determinedly and turned to go.

"You have to get out of the basement," called Tony, but the vampire didn't answer. Tony watched him vanish among the bushes.

Sadly, Tony made his way home. He'd made no progress, and now there was only Wednesday left before he'd promised to tell his mother what was going on in the basement.

"Do you call this seven o'clock?" demanded his mother as he came into the apartment.

"No," he muttered. The evening news was already on television.

"Why are you home so late?"

"I, uh, I was playing hide-and-seek."

"For this long?"

"My hiding place was so good that no one found me till just now."

It wasn't bad for an excuse, and Tony smiled in spite of himself.

"I don't see what's so funny," said his mother angrily. "If it happens again, you won't be allowed outside anymore in the evening."

I won't want to go, thought Tony. At least, not after tomorrow.

After dinner Tony crawled into bed, exhausted. Poor Rudolph, he thought just before he fell asleep, hunting for food every night must be hard work.

21 / Out Hunting

The clock on the church tower struck eight-thirty. Shivering, the little vampire made his way out from behind the trees, where he had been lying hidden for the last half hour. A couple of people had passed, but unfortunately not the right kind. Either they were in pairs, which made an ambush very difficult, or else they reeked of garlic.

However, just then a woman turned the corner alone. The little vampire quickly hid himself behind a telephone pole. Heels tapping, the woman came nearer. She was a tall, strong-looking woman, Rudolph noticed, and she would certainly not be short of blood. She had almost reached the telephone pole when she stopped. An ice-cold shiver ran down Rudolph's spine. Had she noticed him? Cautiously he peered around at the street. A few yards away, the

woman was standing with her back to him. Her hair was held back with a clip, and her coat had only a narrow, flat collar, so the vampire could easily see the pale expanse of her neck. He gave a low moan, and as if drawn by a magnetic force, he crept out from behind the pole.

But at that very moment the woman called out, "King!" and clapped her hands. A huge German shepherd came bounding around the corner, and the little vampire just had time to spring back into the bushes. There he crouched while the dog sniffed around, and finally, as though the vampire had not been through enough already, it lifted its leg against the very bush Rudolph was hiding in.

"Come along, King," said the woman. "We're going home."

The little vampire listened grimly to the sound of her receding footsteps. "What a mess," he grumbled, removing the thorns from his fingers. Although his stomach was growling with hunger, he didn't move. It was the pits being a vampire, and he wasn't ashamed when two tears trickled slowly down his cheeks.

"Look, there's someone crying!" he suddenly heard a voice say.

"He looks so funny," said a second voice.

"Yes, he looks like a vampire," replied the first with a giggle.

In front of him stood two children, each one car-

rying a long stick, at the end of which dangled a
brightly lit lantern. The little vampire quickly wiped
a hand over his wet cheeks.

"What do you want?" he asked, shifting his stiff
legs slightly.

The children were at the most eight years old—not
very appetizing morsels. But still, they'd be better
than nothing. . . .

"Why don't you come along with me?" he suggested in his most friendly voice. "I know a really
dark path where your lanterns will shine much better."

"Where is it?" asked the younger child.

"In the cemetery, of course."

"We'll have to ask our parents first," said the older
of the two.

"Why? It's much more fun without grown-ups,"
said Rudolph persuasively.

"But they're right behind us," said the child, and
called back, "Daddy, Mommy, come here! We found
a real live . . ." But before he could finish, the vampire had vanished.

Rudolph ran to the wall of the cemetery without
turning around once. He jumped over it and let himself fall to the ground with a sigh of relief.

As he looked around him, he was overcome with a
feeling of homesickness, and he thought with longing
of the happy times in the family vault. The oak tree

and the entrance to it were not far away. What he wouldn't give for a glimpse of his old home. He wondered whether the coffins were still where they used to be. Or had they been changed around since his banishment? Maybe Anna slept next to Greg now.

Nothing much could happen if he took one quick look. He was sure that all the vampires would be out hunting at this time of night.

Then suddenly there was a rustling just behind him, and a figure in overalls, with long wooden stakes poking out of the pockets, sprang forward. It was McRookery, the nightwatchman, and he advanced upon Rudolph with a devilish grin.

"At last I've got you, you little rascal!" he said.

Nearer and nearer he came. . . .

"No!" cried Tony. "No!"

He opened his eyes and found he was lying in his bed. Had he been dreaming?

"Tony?" he heard his mother's voice ask. "What's the matter, dear?"

He turned on the light. His mother was sitting on the edge of his bed.

"Are you all right?" she asked.

"Yes," he murmured. "It was just a dream." He shook his head.

"Sleep well, then, sweetheart," said his mother. "We'll talk about it tomorrow if you want."

22 / Heavy Loads

After school the following day, Tony's mother said, "You've been dreaming such terrible dreams lately, Tony. A couple of times I've woken up, because you've cried out in your sleep. And then you start saying funny names like Aunt Dorothy and Gruesome Gregory and Mabel the Mean. . . ."

Tony bit his lip. "Do I really?" he asked innocently.

"Yes. I'm worried about you, Tony," she said, watching her son closely.

So am I, was what Tony would have liked to reply, but he could not admit it, of course. So instead, as if he hadn't a care in the world, he said, "Oh, it's nothing, Mom. I'm perfectly fine, really."

"Do you think so?" asked his mother doubtfully. "Do these terrible dreams have anything to do with your nocturnal expeditions?"

"Wh-what do you m-mean?" stuttered Tony. Did she know about his visit to the Valley of Doom?

"Well," she began, "it just so happens that recently you've been staying out very late—once till almost eight o'clock. What do you do outside for all that time?"

"Play hide-and-seek, like I said."

"Do you really expect me to believe that?"

He shrugged his shoulders.

"And what about the secret in the basement?" she went on.

At once Tony was on the alert. "What about it?"

"Does it have anything to do with your nightmares?"

"No. Nothing at all," said Tony quickly.

"Can I go down to the storeroom now?"

"Now?" asked Tony in horror. "Why?"

"Because I want to find something in one of the old magazines."

"Couldn't it wait until tomorrow?"

"I need to take the article to school tomorrow morning."

Tony thought for a moment. "I'll get it for you."

"Would you really, dear?"

"Of course," said Tony, as though it was the most natural thing in the world.

"I don't know exactly which magazine it's in."

"You don't? Oh. Well, I'll bring them all up."

"Will you?" Tony's mother could not believe her ears. "The whole pile?"

"Yeah—why not?" said Tony. "When do you want them?"

"Well, right now would be wonderful."

And so it happened that ten minutes later Tony could be seen taking the elevator down to the basement. He had pretended everything was fine to his mother, but in fact he could have screamed with frustration—and all because of the little vampire. He opened the storeroom door and turned on the light. The lid of the coffin was closed, and from underneath it he could hear a soft snoring. That's fine, thought Tony, you just sleep tight. You've got me running myself ragged for you, after all. He would have given anything to take the vampire by the shoulders and give him a good shake, and get all his pent-up anger out of his system.

He stood still for a moment, undecided as to what to do. Maybe he'd better take a look at Rudolph. He had read that, during the daytime, vampires sleep like the dead. Carefully, Tony took hold of the coffin lid and pushed it to one side. The head and shoulders of the vampire were now visible. Tony shuddered involuntarily. He had never seen Rudolph look so deathly. His glassy eyes were staring straight ahead and his cheeks had sunken in. Only his mouth,

sagging open slightly with marks of dried blood around it, showed that he was not dead after all.

"Rudolph?" he said quietly.

No answer.

"Rudolph?" he repeated.

The vampire did not move. The smell of decay hung pungently around him and nearly made Tony gag. "Yuck!" he said, and shut the coffin lid. Compared to that, Tony's feet even on their worst day smelled like a bunch of roses.

He began to search for the magazines unenthusiastically. Finally he found them, neatly tied together, by the workbench. How many were in the pile? Fifty? Sixty? A hundred? He took the top fifteen or so. They were heavier than he had imagined. When he reached the storeroom door, he had to put them down in order to close it behind him. Then, arms aching, he lifted them once more.

"Here's the first bunch," he announced, as his mother opened the door of the apartment.

"Oh, Tony," she said, smiling. "You look worn out from all that effort. Are you sure you don't want me to help?"

Tony shook his head vehemently. "It's good exercise," he assured her.

It took him five trips back and forth before he managed to get the whole bunch up to the apartment. Then he fell on his bed, exhausted. His arms felt as if he'd been doing push-ups for a whole hour, and his knees felt like rubber.

"A friend in need is a friend indeed," he said through clenched teeth. That was Grandma's favorite saying, which he had often wondered about. Now he found it was just about true.

To try to take his mind off how annoyed he felt, he took *Voices from the Vault* down from his bookshelf, but he had hardly turned a page before he fell fast asleep.

23 / A Dangerous Plan

When Tony woke up, everything was completely silent in the apartment. He looked at his watch: it was almost six o'clock. Somehow he must have dozed off, and been asleep for more than two hours! How could he, today of all days, when every minute counted?

He sprang out of bed and went to the bedroom door. At six o'clock Mom was almost always in the kitchen getting supper ready, but today there was no clinking of cutlery, no music on the radio—had she gone out?

Quietly Tony opened his door. Even then he couldn't hear anything, so he made his way on tiptoe across the hallway. No one was there. On the kitchen table there was a note:

Dear Tony,

I've gone to meet Dad at the office. There's a little party going on there this evening. Give yourself supper, and be sure to be back in the apartment by seven-thirty at the latest—we'll give you a call at eight o'clock.

Love,
Mom

He let the note drop. A miracle had occurred! His parents would be out for the whole evening, and he could stay away for as long as it took to bring this matter to a close once and for all. Tony gave a little jump of satisfaction.

His stomach gurgled, and he remembered that he hadn't had anything to eat. He cut himself a slice of bread and smeared it liberally with butter, then put a thick slice of cheese on top.

While he chewed, he thought feverishly of what he should do. Go down to the basement and try to talk to Rudolph again? He might listen this time. However, he soon discarded this plan. He only had to imagine Rudolph sitting yawning in his coffin, complaining how hungry he was, to realize there must be a better solution.

What if he tried to find Anna? She would certainly sympathize with him and help try to find a way out.

At the thought of Anna, Tony began to feel better.

His plan had only one drawback: The only place he could be sure of meeting her was at the vault. He would have to lie in wait near the entrance until she came out. . . . He gave a shudder at the thought of all the other vampires who would certainly be coming out that way too. But it was a risk he would have to take. And just in case, he would hang his mother's silver chain with the crucifix around his neck and put a few garlic cloves in his pocket.

He looked out the kitchen window. It was still light, but soon it would be dusk, and by then he had to be at the cemetery. He took the necklace out of his mother's jewelry box, broke off four cloves of garlic, and left.

24 / The Open Door

By the entrance door, Tony ran into Mrs. Tatum. She had her dachshund on a leash, and the dog began to bark loudly when she caught sight of Tony. Mrs. Tatum threw him a look and walked stiffly past without responding to his greeting.

"Your dog used to be more polite!" he called after Mrs. Tatum, which only made the dachshund bark more frenziedly. Mrs. Tatum dragged her, still protesting, into the hallway with an anxious look upward at her neighbors' windows.

The world is *full* of vampires, mused Tony, and the ones with pointed teeth aren't always the worst kind.

Luckily he didn't meet anybody else he knew, and so came without incident to the cemetery. It lay silent and deserted, and Tony was able to make his way undisturbed to the main pathway. Here the hedges were trimmed and the graves well cared for, quite different from the other side of the cemetery, where everything was overgrown, and the vampires' vault was to be found.

As he approached the chapel at the end of the path, he noticed that its huge, iron-studded door stood open.

Tony stood rooted to the spot in horror. He could hear his heart beating, and he clutched involuntarily at the chain around his neck. Who or what was out and about in the chapel? While he debated whether to turn back or go on, a man came out of it, shut the door behind him, and locked it with a large padlock. It was McRookery, the nightwatchman. The long face, the large nose, and the overalls with wooden stakes and a hammer poking out of the pockets could only belong to him. He knew well enough that the only way to get rid of a vampire is to drive a wooden stake through its heart.

By now, McRookery had spied Tony. His face adopted a black expression and he came toward him with long, slow strides. It was just like his dream, in which he had imagined McRookery was about to catch Rudolph, and Tony felt the sweat break out on his forehead. Any minute now, McRookery would lift the hammer, and then . . .

But instead, McRookery peered at him in an unfriendly way with his eyes and said, "What are you up to, my boy?" His breath smelled so strongly of garlic that Tony almost had to hold his nose.

"I—I was just passing through," Tony stammered. He took a couple of steps backward. "I-it's my shortcut home."

"Is it, now?" It was clear Mr. McRookery did not believe a word of it. "You're going the wrong way for the gate."

He took the stakes out of his pocket and ran his thumb thoughtfully over their pointed ends. Tony felt goose pimples rise on his skin.

"I'm on my way," he said, and turned around and ran off down the main path all the way to the gate without stopping. Only then did he dare to look back. McRookery was following him, but did not seem to be in any great hurry. In his hand he carried a large ring of keys, and Tony supposed he was going to lock the main gate after him. Quickly Tony went through it and leaned against the wall on the other side, which was smooth and newly painted. A pine tree hid him from McRookery's view, and so he had a couple of minutes to catch his breath and think. It was already beginning to get dark—exactly the time for him to be at the vault.

Since McRookery had barred the way through the graveyard, there was only one choice. He would have to climb over the wall in the back. Not a very pleasant prospect, because he could easily meet a

vampire coming over it the other way. And if he met
a vampire before he had time to hide behind one of
the gravestones near the entrance to the vault . . . He
did not let himself think about that, but ran till he

reached the gray, crumbling part of the wall at the back of the cemetery. He looked quickly around on all sides, and when he saw nothing suspicious, he got a foothold on a stone and hoisted himself over the top.

25 / The Vampires Are Coming

This particular part of the cemetery had always given Tony the creeps. The grass grew knee-high, and overturned gravestones and twisted crosses gave the place an air of ghostliness. He was even more aware of it today than usual, and he looked anxiously over to the tall oak tree, under which the entrance to the vault lay hidden. Was there something moving over there? Tony's mouth felt dry, and he ducked swiftly behind one of the tombstones. His heart was beating so fast he thought it must be audible to the dark figure that now emerged from under the shadow of the oak.

It was a small, squat vampire. He looked around long and searchingly before finally spreading his arms under his cape and flying away. Tony breathed a sigh of relief, because the vampire had looked hard in his direction more than once. There followed a second figure—a tall, strong-looking vampire who flew off without any hesitation. Could it have been Gruesome Gregory?

Then the stone at the vault's entrance grated a little, and Tony held his breath. A small, slender vampire, bent over a stick, came hobbling out of the shadows. Tony heard her groan softly. Then she hid her stick under the folds of her cape and flew away. Was it Sabina the Sinister?

Once more the branches of the oak tree moved gently, and yet another figure came forward. It stood still and sniffed the air curiously. Tony's heart missed a beat: The figure was looking straight at him! Yes, there was no doubt about it, it had seen him. Now it was coming closer with swift strides—it was Aunt Dorothy. Tony was paralyzed with fear. His whole body was trembling, and he stared straight back at her, unable to move a muscle. By now she was so close, he could see her mouth, gaping wide.

"No!" he croaked in terror.

"Why ever not?" he heard Aunt Dorothy saying. "It only hurts a little bit at first. After that it's very nice." She reached out for him, and Tony could feel her cold, deathly breath.

"Please," he whispered. He wondered why she wasn't reacting to the garlic in his pocket.

"You mustn't struggle so, sweetie," said Aunt Dorothy. "Otherwise I'll miss, and you'll get terrible scars."

Tony thought he was about to faint. Suddenly, the stone at the vault's entrance scraped back once more, and a familiar clear voice called, "Aunt Dorothy, what are you doing?"

Aunt Dorothy hesitated. "What do you want?" she asked in surprise.

Tony opened his eyes and recognized Anna. A stab of relief shot through him. Maybe all was not lost after all.

"Aunt Dorothy, you're wanted downstairs at once," he heard Anna say.

"Downstairs, my dear? Why?" Aunt Dorothy was definitely distrustful.

"You're going to be rewarded for finding out about Rudolph. But you've got to hurry up."

Aunt Dorothy looked pleased, but then her look changed to one of greed. "What about him?" she asked, pointing at Tony.

"I'll keep an eye on him for you," said Anna.

"All right, then, my dear," said Aunt Dorothy, casting one last longing look at Tony's neck before heading toward the vault. "You keep your hands off him, now," she called back over her shoulder, obviously forgetting that Anna was not old enough for blood yet, and drank only milk.

Once she had disappeared, Anna seized Tony by the arm. "Come on, we've got to run," she urged.

"What about Aunt Dorothy?" asked Tony, who was still numb.

"That's the point! She'll be back any minute, and if she finds you here . . ." She said no more, but pulled Tony after her toward the wall of the cemetery. Tony followed as if in a dream. His head was swimming, and he still felt under the spell of Aunt Dorothy's eyes, which had held him captive.

"We can't waste any time," said Anna once they were safely over the wall. "Aunt Dorothy can fly, and we've only got one cape between us."

"Wh-where should we go?" asked Tony.

"As far away as possible," said Anna, "till Aunt Dorothy's given up looking for us."

26 / On the Run

"Why can't we hide?" asked Tony.

"Where?" said Anna.

"Back at my house?"

Anna shook her head. "Aunt Dorothy knows where you live."

"What about in the school, then?"

"In your school?" Anna stopped still and looked at him. With great deliberation, she looked up at the sky and asked, "And just how do you propose we're going to hide in there? It's locked up, isn't it?"

Tony grinned. "It is," he said. "But my house key fits the main entrance lock also."

"It does?" said Anna with a slow smile. "I've always wanted to see what a school looks like on the inside."

It wasn't long before they reached the school. Next

to it, in a small house belonging to the janitor, a light was burning, but otherwise all was in darkness.

"I'll go first," whispered Tony. He climbed over the wooden fence and Anna followed him. They crept across the schoolyard, which looked strange and unfamiliar in the darkness, till they came to the long, low building. Tony pulled a bunch of keys out of his pocket, while Anna kept watch for Aunt Dorothy.

"Can you see her?" asked Tony anxiously.

"I don't know," replied Anna. "There's something moving over there, but whether it's Aunt Dorothy or not..."

By now Tony had the key in the lock and the door opened. They quickly slipped inside and shut it behind them. Then they stood still and listened.

"Can you hear anything?" asked Tony.

"Yes," answered Anna softly. "There *is* something creeping around out there."

Tony couldn't hear anything, but he broke out in goose pimples anyway.

"A-Aunt Dorothy?" he stammered.

"Maybe."

Several minutes passed, which seemed like an eternity to Tony. Finally Anna announced, "She's gone."

"Was it Aunt Dorothy?"

"Yes," replied Anna. "Didn't you hear her teeth chattering?"

At the thought that Aunt Dorothy was even now only a few yards away, Tony's hair stood on end. "Do you think she knows we're in here?" he asked.

"I'm sure she doesn't," Anna reassured him. "Otherwise she wouldn't have gone away."

Tony felt as though a weight had dropped from his shoulders. At last he'd be able to talk to Anna about Rudolph in peace.

27 / In Tony's Classroom

But Anna seemed to be interested in other things for
the time being.

"Which is your classroom?" she asked excitedly.

"The one on the left," answered Tony.

She had already opened the door. "Come on," she
called.

"You know, Anna, I've got to talk to you . . ."
began Tony.

"Yes, yes," she said carelessly. "In a minute. Right
now I'm much too curious." She ran around the
room, counting the desks by the light of the moon.

"Thirty-six," she exclaimed. "How sociable!"

"You call that sociable?" Tony was shocked. "Do
you think it's good that you only get attention once
every class?"

"Of course it is," said Anna. "Then you can go to sleep for the rest of the time."

"You'd get an F for that kind of work," replied Tony.

Anna had stopped by the teacher's desk. "Whose is this huge desk?" she asked.

"My teacher's." Tony was beginning to feel the inspection had gone on long enough.

"I see," said Anna musingly. "That's so she can frighten all the children, isn't it?" She bent down and looked in all the drawers. "But she doesn't have any whips," she said disappointedly.

"Whipping isn't allowed anymore," explained Tony.

"It isn't?" asked Anna. "But Greg always says . . ."

"They have much better ways nowadays," said Tony.

Anna thought for a moment. "Like what?" she asked.

"Grades."

"Grades?" Anna didn't understand. "How do they work?"

"Very simple," answered Tony. "At school you get grades for everything. If you get good ones, you can go on to a 'selective' college, as my parents call them, and later you'll get a good job and earn lots of money. But if you get bad grades—"

"But that's unfair!" interrupted Anna. "What if you can't help having a hard time with the work?"

"I know," agreed Tony.

"What kind of grades do you get?"

"Medium."

"Will you get into a 'selective' school?"

"Got me. Depends if I want to," replied Tony.

Anna looked thoughtfully out the window. "Maybe it isn't as great at school as I'd thought," she said. Then something else occurred to her. "Where's your desk?"

"This one," said Tony, pointing to a desk in the second-to-last row.

"Who sits next to you?" asked Anna. "Not a—girl, I hope?"

Tony had to smile. "No—a boy," he reassured her.

Anna breathed a sigh of relief. "Come and sit in your chair for a moment," she said.

"Why?" asked Tony, sitting down.

"Because I'd like to sit next to you," she said, and smiled. "Now it's like we were school friends," she said wistfully, sitting down next to him. "I'd see you every morning in school, we could go to the playground together every day, and in the evenings we'd do our homework together. . . ." Her voice trailed off sadly, and she wiped her eyes with the back of her hand. "Oh, Tony," she said, and turned her huge swimming eyes right on him. Tony turned his head away quickly.

"I need to talk to you about Rudolph," he said, to hide his embarrassment.

"Rudolph!" she exclaimed. "You obviously don't find *me* very interesting."

"No, it's not that," Tony assured her. Whatever happened, he better not annoy her. But how was he supposed to find the right words with Anna sobbing away, and he himself feeling so weird?

"You see, Anna," he began, "it's about those panels of wood."

"Panels of wood?" she asked.

"The ones in the basement. Grandpa's coming tomorrow, and he and Dad are going to go down and get them."

"No!" exclaimed Anna. "What about poor Rudolph? How can he get his coffin back to the vault in time? It's true that the ban has been lifted, but—"

"Lifted?" Tony could hardly believe his ears. "The ban's been lifted?" His voice trembled with relief.

"Yes—it was this morning."

"Well, then . . ." Words almost failed Tony. "He can go back to the vault tonight!"

"What about his coffin?" Anna reminded him. "He won't be able to take that away by himself. In any case, I'm sure he's gone out by now."

"We could carry the coffin."

"What if Rudolph comes back and finds his coffin's gone?"

"We'll leave a note on the basement window," said Tony. Anna looked away. "Please, Anna," he begged.

She looked sideways at him and gave a little smile. "When you ask like that, how can I refuse?"

Tony almost spread out his arms and gave her a hug, but he stopped himself just in time and gave her a friendly nudge instead. "You're the greatest," he said, and for once he meant it.

"Do you really think so?" she asked, and though there was only the light of the moon to see by, Tony realized she had turned a deep red.

"Anyhow," she said, changing the subject, "someone in your class stinks."

"Do you think so?" Apart from Anna's slightly musty smell, he hadn't noticed anything.

"Yes," she said firmly, and her mouth turned down at the corners. "A really revolting smell of—garlic!"

"Garlic?" echoed Tony. Then he suddenly remembered the pieces of garlic he had hidden in his pockets. Hesitantly, he delved into them and brought out the garlic.

Anna gave a shriek. "No! Put them away! Do you want to make me sick?"

"S-sorry," stuttered Tony, "I didn't realize..."

"Don't you know the old vampire saying

Beware of garlic. 'Tis so strong
'Twill give you cramps the whole day long."

Anna had retreated to the other side of the desk. "Quickly, get rid of the stuff."

Tony opened the window and threw it out into the playground.

"I brought it in case I met Aunt Dorothy," he explained. "But it didn't seem to do any good."

"Of course not," said Anna. "It probably just made her more angry. Her stomach's like a rock."

Tony shuddered. "What about this crucifix?" he asked, showing her the chain around his neck.

Anna dismissed it. "Pure superstition. Only one thing helps, in fact."

"What's that?"

"To be a vampire yourself," said Anna, and giggled.

28 / Painful Progress

On the way home, Tony said, "I really can't believe the ban has been lifted." It seemed like a miracle to him.

"At first it was supposed to be extended to four weeks," explained Anna. "My grandmother, Sabina the Sinister, was especially big on that—as a warning to us other young vampires, she thought. But when I told them all that Rudolph hadn't eaten for days, and was wandering around the place feeling sorry for himself, they began to be afraid that he might lie out in the sun one day in total despair, and expire—so they decided to let him come back to the vault."

"Do you think he would have done that?" asked Tony, worrying. He thought of how weak and sick the young vampire had looked each time he had gone to see him. Maybe Tony hadn't been taking the situation seriously enough.

Anna tried to put his fears to rest. "Don't look so upset," she said, smiling. "I always like to exaggerate."

But Tony couldn't help wondering about it all. What if Rudolph had almost starved because of him? And what about Anna? He looked at her closely. What if the senior vampires decided to banish her now? After all, she must be in the same position as Rudolph.

"What about—I mean, you're in contact with humans as well," he said.

"Oh, they'd never catch me," said Anna scornfully, and, linking her arm with Tony's, she added, "It's nice of you to worry about me, anyway."

Tony coughed to hide his embarrassment. He wished Anna didn't always show her feelings so openly. He carefully removed his arm from hers and said, "We're almost there."

"Are your parents home?" asked Anna.

"No," Tony replied, "and they won't be back before ten, that's for sure. But they're going to call at eight." He suddenly remembered this, and looked at his watch in horror: It was already ten after eight.

"I've got to hurry!" he said. "Do you want to come too?"

"If I'm allowed," said Anna, laughing.

They had barely shut the front door of the apartment behind them when the telephone rang.

"Oh, hi, Mom," said Tony, trying to speak normally even though his heart was hammering against his ribs. "Where was I at eight o'clock?" He looked across at Anna, who was brushing her hair in front of the mirror in the hall. Why did she insist on standing within hearing distance? And anyway, in all the vampire stories he'd ever read, vampires weren't supposed to have reflections.

"I was, er, in the bathroom," he lied.

Anna laughed.

"Well, of course I'm by myself, Mom. Who was that laughing? It was, um, someone on the radio." He gestured frantically to Anna to go into the living room, but she stayed happily where she was and continued to brush her hair.

"Yes, Mom, I'm going right to bed, Mom," he said. Anna laughed again.

"No!" said Tony emphatically into the receiver. "There's no one here. It's a funny show on the radio. Have I washed yet? Yes, Mom. Good night, Mom."

Totally out of breath, he hung up. "She almost was on to you," he said to Anna reproachfully.

"I can't help it if you make me laugh," she retorted. She put down the brush and turned around.

"Do I look pretty?" she asked.

"Ye-yes," he stammered.

"Are you—going to bed now?" she asked.

"No!" Tony growled. "We ought to go and get the coffin," he added hastily.

"Already?" Anna sounded disappointed. "You said your parents wouldn't be back till ten. . . ."

"They might come back earlier."

"Okay." She looked downcast. "If you really think so."

Tony gulped. Had he been thoughtless again?

"I—I've got a book for you," he said to cheer her up. He went into his room and got *Voices from the Vault*. Giving it a last longing look—he had only read half of it—he handed it to her.

"Thank you," said Anna, sounding really pleased,

and she put it into the folds of her cape. "Is it for me?"

"Yes."

"Okay, then, let's go and get that coffin."

"Anna," Tony began as they went down in the elevator together. "Is it true that vampires don't have a reflection?"

Anna looked ashamed and lowered her head. "Do I look so awful?"

"No, no," Tony reassured her. "I was just interested."

"Vampires get such a crummy deal," she complained. "Not only do we have to sleep in worm-eaten old coffins, and wear these smelly old clothes, but we can't even look in a mirror when we want to fix ourselves up a little bit."

Tony tended to agree with her, although he didn't say so out loud. He imagined she'd look very nice in jeans and a sweater, with her hair nicely brushed and a healthier color in her cheeks. . . . He was glad when the elevator stopped, so he didn't have time to finish those thoughts.

"But you don't mind that I look like this, do you?" she asked shyly.

"O-of course not," said Tony. It occurred to him what a good thing it was that the lighting in the basement was so dim—he was definitely blushing.

Tony opened the door to the basement hallway and turned on the light. The smell of mold and decay was even stronger, and he had to smile when he thought of Mrs. Tatum and her sensitive nose. Soon she'd be able to breathe again.

"That one's ours," he said in a whisper, although they were quite alone.

"It stinks," said Anna, giggling.

Tony opened the door and they went in. Everything was as before. The wood was up against the wall, and Rudolph's coffin was half hidden behind it, with its lid propped open.

"Not too cozy," remarked Anna. "And very lonely. Poor Rudolph."

"What?" said Tony angrily. He had had a ton of worries and problems since he had given the little vampire a home, and all Anna could say was "Poor Rudolph!" "Maybe I should have rolled out the red carpet for him," he said sarcastically.

Anna laughed. "No, no. But I was just thinking that for a vampire like Rudolph, who has always lain —um—lived—with other vampires . . ."

"I guess you think I should have come down here to live with him?" asked Tony. He had torn one corner off a cardboard box, and on it he had written in pencil:

Dear Rudolph,

The ban has been lifted. We've taken your coffin back to the vault.

See you,
Tony

He pushed the note between two of the bars on the window grating and shut the window from the inside. Then he began to clear away the wood.

"Can I help?" asked Anna.

"You could put the lid back on the coffin."

Together they lifted the lid. It was so heavy it made Tony's shoulders ache. He looked over at Anna worriedly. How in the world was he going to get both the coffin and the lid all the way to the vault? Anna was shorter than him by a head, and if *he* was having difficulty . . .

But Anna smiled confidently, as though she had guessed his thoughts. "I'm pretty strong," she said, "stronger than Rudolph."

"Are you?" Tony didn't believe her.

To prove it, she lifted the coffin from the middle.

"That's great!" Tony was amazed. "I'd never have guessed."

"No, you wouldn't have," said Anna proudly.

She went to the foot of the coffin, Tony picked up the head, and carefully they carried it to the door.

29 / Three on One Coffin

Luckily, there was nobody around to catch them—so far. After they'd gone through the storeroom door, they carefully put the coffin down, and Tony quickly locked the door behind them. His stomach felt queasy: If they met someone coming down to the basement, or on the way to the cemetery, it would be curtains for sure.

Anna broke into these thoughts with a whispered "Hurry up!" and they picked up the coffin once more.

Without turning on the light, they proceeded along the hallway and up the stairs—the coffin would have never fit in the elevator. Since everything was still quiet when they reached the front door, they took the coffin outside and put it down in the shadow of some bushes.

"Phew!" said Tony, rubbing his aching wrists.

"Not exhausted already, are you?" teased Anna, who seemed as fresh as ever.

"No," said Tony, "not at all." Even if he *had* been, he certainly wouldn't admit it in front of her. "Let's get going," he said, and they set off again. They chose the unlit path across the playground, and reached the street without meeting anybody. Nearly all the cars were parked in their places, and no one was to be seen.

"They're all watching T.V., I bet," said Tony.

"I know," agreed Anna. "When the prime-time shows are on, it's pointless for a vampire to go out hunting."

"What do you do instead?"

"We fly from house to house looking for a way in," she said, giggling.

"Ugh!" said Tony, involuntarily feeling his neck. Just think how many times they left the window open at home. If Aunt Dorothy knew about that . . .

"Should we go on?" asked Anna.

Once again they lifted the coffin and carried it along the sidewalk. Suddenly a figure emerged on the other side of the street. It was a man, and he was walking very unsteadily. He looked across at them curiously.

"Do you know him?" asked Anna.

Tony shook his head. "He's drunk," he explained. The man tottered slowly across the street and came toward them. Tony's knees began to knock. Should they run off and leave the coffin? But then what would happen to it? The same thought seemed to have occurred to Anna, because she whispered, "Let's just put it down and sit on it. Then he won't see it."

She jumped onto the coffin and spread out her cape, and Tony sat down next to her. By now the man was close enough for Tony to smell the beer on his breath. He sneezed.

"Well, children, move over a tad," the man said. "Make room for your ol' uncle—hic!"

Tony and Anna exchanged horrified glances.

"Or ishn't that a bench?" The man stooped down to examine the coffin more closely, lost his balance, and toppled heavily against it.

"If I washn't so drunk, I'd shay that was a coffin." The man peered at Tony and Anna through red-rimmed eyes. "Ish that a bench, or isn't it a—hic—bench?" he asked.

"I-it's a bench," stammered Tony.

"Well, then." The man sat down heavily and pulled a bottle of beer out of his pocket. "Cheersh," he said, and took a gulp. Then he wiped the rim of the bottle with his thumb and offered it to Anna. "Here, have a drink."

"No thanks," said Anna.

"What about you, shunny?" he said to Tony. "You'll have a shwig, won'tcha?"

"I—I don't like b-beer," said Tony.

"Don't like beer?" The man was amazed. "Well, well. When I was a kid like you . . ." He tilted back the bottle and took another long drink. "You'll have one of these though, won'tcha—hic?" he added, and offered Tony a cigarette. Tony shook his head. "Don't shmoke neither?" The man looked mystified. "How'll you ever learn to, unless you try it?"

"I don't want to learn how to," Tony told him.

The man drained the bottle and flung it into a bush. Then, with trembling fingers, he tried to light his cigarette, and once this was accomplished, he leaned back contentedly—and fell over backward with a crash. He looked so funny that Anna began to laugh.

"Ssssh!" hissed Tony. "You shouldn't make fun of drunk people. I think we'd better scram before he gets up."

They picked up the coffin and raced off.

"Hey, wait," the man called after them. "You tricked me! That's no bench. Benches have backs."

He wobbled to his feet with difficulty and took a couple of faltering steps toward them, but they were already so far away that he didn't try to follow them.

30 / Mixed Feelings

"Will you drink beer when you grow up?" asked Anna.

"Definitely not as much as that man," replied Tony.

"Why did he drink so much?"

"He probably had problems and wanted to forget them. . . ."

"Oh," said Anna.

At last they could see the cemetery wall jutting up in the darkness. Tony breathed a sigh of relief. His hands had lost most of their feeling, and his back ached. Anna, on the other hand, carried the coffin with an ease that looked as if she could have gone on all night.

"Just a little bit farther," she said encouragingly.

"Mmmm," mumbled Tony.

They turned off down a narrow path. "The best place to get the coffin over is here," said Anna. Tony had mixed feelings. The thick bushes on either side of the path were an ideal hiding place—for Aunt Dorothy, for instance. . . . But they reached the wall without incident, put down the coffin, and Anna whispered, "I'll go over first, and you can heave the coffin over to me." She scrambled up and over the wall, which was so high that Tony found he could just barely reach the top by stretching up his arms.

"Why couldn't we have tried nearer to the vault?" he asked. "The wall's much lower there."

"Too dangerous," explained Anna. "Think of Mc-Rookery."

Tony looked helplessly from the coffin to the wall. They'd never make it.

"Ready!" called Anna.

Tony put his hands under the coffin and tried to lift it. "I can't," he said.

"Try the lid first," whispered Anna.

Tony got a good grip on the lid and heaved it with all his strength over the top of the wall.

"Got it?" he asked.

"No," said Anna, but it was too late. Tony lost his hold, and the lid fell with a crash down the other side. There was a sharp cry.

"Are you okay?" called Tony anxiously.

"No!" came the answer.

"Want me to come and help?"

"No!"

While Tony was thinking what he should do next, Anna climbed back with effort over the wall. Her face was streaked with tears, and she held one foot out.

"Is it broken?" Tony was shocked.

"No," she growled, and furiously picked up the rest of the coffin and pulled it up the wall. Tony watched her helplessly.

"Grab hold," she ordered, and immediately Tony reached for the lower end. As Anna climbed up and over the wall, Tony did his best to keep the coffin steady.

"Should I push?" he asked.

"NO!" she said, and pulled the heavy coffin over with her. Tony heard her put the lid on again.

"Are you mad?" he asked.

"Yes," she said, and added bitterly, "Klutz!"

"I didn't do it on purpose."

There was no answer.

"Anna, I'm sorry. Please!"

Still no answer. Surely she hadn't gone off alone with the coffin? Tony put one foot on a stone and pulled himself up till he could just see over the top of the wall. Dimly he could make out Anna carrying the

coffin through the long grass. She stumbled, and he heard her moan softly.

"Anna," he called. "Don't go away. I didn't mean to hurt you."

But she went on.

"Anna," he called again, but she had disappeared into the trees.

Tony slid down from the wall and stood still, uncertain. Then he turned around and headed back home. It was funny—this time he never gave a thought to the bushes and the danger that might be lurking behind them. He kept seeing Anna, struggling through the grass with the coffin, and not turning around to look at him. It gave him a funny feeling in his stomach, as if he had eaten too much popcorn and candy. Was this what it felt like to be in love? The other strange thing was that, although he should have been feeling mighty relieved to be rid of the coffin at last, he didn't. All he felt was that he had behaved like a bull in a china shop, and he didn't blame Anna for being so furious.

He reached the apartment building, took the elevator upstairs, and unlocked the door. No one was home yet.

He fell onto the bed with a heavy heart. Will she ever forgive me? he thought as he went to sleep.

31 / All for Nothing

"Tony!" His mother's voice seemed to come from far away. "Tony, get up!"

"Mmmm," he mumbled.

"Tony, it's already seven-fifteen."

He rubbed his eyes and blinked. His mother had turned on the light, and it blinded him. All his limbs ached, and he groaned as he turned away.

"Are you sick?" his mother asked anxiously.

"Sick?" Now that was a good idea! And to be honest, he didn't feel particularly well. He put on a woeful expression.

"I think I've got the flu."

"Flu?" His mother was concerned and felt his forehead. "You don't feel like you have a fever."

"I ache all over," he moaned.

"We'd better take your temperature, then," said his

mother. She disappeared into the bathroom and came back with the thermometer.

"Here you go—and no funny business."

"What do you mean, funny business?" asked Tony, sounding hurt. Nevertheless, his mother stayed sitting on the edge of his bed and timed him with her watch.

"Tony, you aren't wearing your pajamas," she said suddenly.

"A-aren't I?" Tony was surprised himself, and he quickly drew the covers up to his chin.

"No," she said, gesturing to his chair. "You only took off your sweater and pants . . . and what do your clothes smell of, anyway?" She held Tony's sweater suspiciously under her nose.

"Um, a little campfire," said Tony quickly.

"Campfire?"

"Yes, we made one yesterday."

Mrs. Noodleman did not look convinced, but the three minutes were up, so she contented herself with taking the thermometer.

"Ninety-eight point five," she said. "Can't call that a temperature."

"But I feel so lousy. . . ."

"Who's going to look after you if you stay at home?"

"Dad's here today, and so's Grandpa." There was no way Tony could forget that today was the day

146

they were going to work on the kitchen—and needed the wooden panels from the basement.

"Dad? He left for the office a long time ago."

"But he was going to . . ." said Tony, and stopped, puzzled. "I thought he and Grandpa were going to start on the kitchen today."

"They were. But something came up."

Tony felt his eyes fill with tears, and he had to bite his lip to keep from letting out a howl. He'd nearly killed himself trying to get the coffin out of the basement in time, and then when he *did* manage it, "something came up"! What a mean thing to let happen.

"It's not that bad," said his mother, smoothing back his hair. "Everyone's sick from time to time."

If only that were the problem, he thought, and turned his face to the wall with a sob.

"You can stay in bed for today, and I'll make you some nice tea and toast," said his mother. "But then I have to be going."

When she'd left the room, Tony lay in bed and stared up at the ceiling. He really did have bad luck. On the other hand, at least the coffin wasn't in the basement anymore, so he had no real need to worry when his parents announced they had to get something from the storeroom.

He sighed deeply once more, then crept under the covers and, not very long after that, was fast asleep.

32 / All Is Revealed

When his mother came back at lunchtime, Tony was sitting up in bed. He had put a couple of extra pillows behind his back, and was reading.

"Hi, Mom," he said, smiling.

"You look much better," she replied.

"Well, yeah," he said, a little shamefacedly. He would rather not admit that he'd just been dead tired, and overanxious about his dad's plans.

"What's for lunch?" he asked. He was starving after the exertions of the evening before.

"Piping hot stew," answered his mother, "but I'll have to go down to the basement for the potatoes."

"Okay," he said, and a feeling of great contentment stole over him. Now it was all the same to him whether she went down to the basement or not. Suddenly he noticed she was looking at him in surprise.

"Don't you mind if I go down there?" she asked.

"No," replied Tony. "Why should I?"

She smiled. "When I needed to search through all those old magazines down there, you wouldn't let me near the place. So has your secret disappeared?"

"My secret?" Tony couldn't help laughing, although he tried hard. All he had to do now was explain everything to his mother. "The vampire's moved out," he said.

"The—what?"

"The vampire who's been living in our storeroom," explained Tony.

"You and your vampires," scolded his mother, shaking her head. "Was it such a terrible secret that now you can't tell me the truth?"

"Don't you think that a vampire who's been banned from his family vault is a terrible-enough secret?" replied Tony.

"Vampires, vampires!" As always when this subject came up, his mother's voice became impatient. "Can't you get interested in something more sensible?"

"Of course," said Tony with a grin. "Last week in the library, I picked a book on werewolves instead."

"Hmph," said his mother, and went out of the room. Tony laughed quietly to himself. As he'd expected, she hadn't believed a word of it—luckily! He heard the front door close, and then it was just a short time before the key turned in the lock again.

His mother came straight back into his bedroom. In her hand she carried a basket of potatoes—and the vampire's toothbrush.

"What is this?" she asked, examining the brush in obvious mystification. It was almost bald, and the few bristles it did have were twisted and stubby.

"I—um—don't know," stuttered Tony.

"Eeugh!" said his mother, throwing it into the wastepaper basket. "Someone must have pushed it under the door. And what an odor there is down there!" She took a potato out of the basket and smelled it. "I hope these are all right."

On that note, she went into the kitchen. Tony immediately sprang out of bed and rescued the toothbrush from the scraps of paper in the wastepaper basket. He hid it under his pillow and leaned back contentedly.

"Will you call me when lunch is ready?" he said.

33 / Nocturnal Gratitude

"Tomorrow, it's back to school for you, and I don't want to hear another word about it," said Mrs. Noodleman firmly that evening.

"Mmm," said Tony, hoping he sounded sick. There was no way his mother was going to be taken in, though.

"If you were really feeling bad, you'd be asleep by now," she pointed out.

Tony stole a glance at the clock. It was almost eight. "Yeah, well, I am sort of tired," he said with an exaggerated yawn. In fact he was wide-awake—understandably, since he had slept until lunchtime. But the best thing to do would be to go to his room, get into bed, and read until he felt sleepy. "Good night," he said.

"Night, sleep tight," answered his father from the bathroom, where he was busy hanging up shirts to dry.

"Sleep well, dear," said his mother.

Once in his room, Tony closed the curtains, put on his pajamas, and crept into bed. He thought longingly of the book about werewolves that he had described to his mother. That would have been the perfect thing to read tonight to help him fall asleep. But unfortunately it still stood on the shelves of "Adult Reading Material," which Tony was not yet allowed to take out of the library. What was more, he had given *Voices from the Vault* to Anna. The only thing left to do was to reread one of his old books. He had just chosen *Twelve Chilling Vampire Tales* from his bookshelf when there came a gentle tapping on the windowpane. Tony jumped in fear. Aunt Dorothy! After all, she did know where he lived. . . .

He tiptoed over to the window and peered through the crack between the curtains. On the windowsill sat the little vampire, smiling in a friendly sort of way.

"You?" Tony was surprised. He'd thought of all the other vampires—Aunt Dorothy, Gruesome Greg, Anna—but he'd never thought it would be Rudolph. Rudolph had already had one banishment because of him.

"My parents are here," he warned, opening the window and letting the little vampire in.

"What are they doing?" asked Rudolph.

"Watching the news on television."

"That's okay." The little vampire relaxed visibly. "They won't bother us."

"What in the world are you doing here? Aren't you scared that Aunt Dorothy will catch you again?" Tony asked.

"Yes, but I've come for Anna's sake this time."

"Anna?" Tony felt himself redden.

"Yes. She said that whatever else I did, I had to come and thank you."

Tony's face turned even more red. "What for?" he asked.

"Well, because you've been so hospitable and let me stay in your basement. . . ."

"Oh, that!" Tony sighed with relief. For a moment he thought that Rudolph had come to try and straighten out the fight he'd had with Anna. But luckily the little vampire did not seem to know anything about it.

"It was nothing," he said magnanimously. "You would've done the same for me."

"Yes." The little vampire nodded eagerly. "You can come and stay with me anytime you want"—he paused—"but you'd have to turn into a vampire first."

That gave Tony a scare. "Vampire?" he said with a shudder, suddenly thinking that Rudolph's smile looked more than a bit menacing. "I don't *want* to be a vampire."

"Don't you?" Rudolph paused again. "Not even for —Anna?"

"No," said Tony, trying to keep his voice from shaking. "Anyway, we had a fight."

"I know."

"Did Anna tell you?"

"Yes. And she said I should ask you something about it."

Tony blushed again.

"She asked me to ask you whether you were still mad at her."

Tony could hardly keep from laughing out loud. Whether *he* was still mad at *her*? "No!" he said, and a great weight slipped from him. "I'm not mad at her."

"Really not?" asked Rudolph.

"No," said Tony.

"That's good, then," said the little vampire, and with these words he went right over to the window and pulled back the curtains. There, on the far corner of the windowsill, sat Anna, all wrapped up in the cape.

"All's well," explained Rudolph. "You can come in, but keep it quiet."

Gracefully, Anna uncurled herself and slipped into the room.

"Hi there, Tony!" she said.

About the Author

Angela Sommer-Bodenburg is the author of numerous short stories that have appeared in magazines and anthologies throughout the world, as well as several collections of poetry. Ms. Sommer-Bodenburg introduced readers to Tony and Rudolph the vampire in *My Friend the Vampire*, recently published by Dial.